THE CHILD IN THE HOUSE
and Other Imaginary Portraits
by Walter Pater

With an Introduction by May Ottley
Annotated by R.J. Allinson

Noumena Press
Whately, Massachusetts
www.noumenapress.com

Noumena Classics are published by Noumena Press
Printed by Lightning Source on acid-free paper
Distributed worldwide by Ingram

Version 2.0
Formerly published by Noumena Press as
Three Imaginary Portraits

ISBN-13: 9780976706212 (paperback)
LCCN: 2017959745

Also available as a PDF e-book
Visit www.noumenapress.com for details

Cover: altered detail of an untitled daguerreotype [Boy with Parrot, c. 1856] by Antoine Claudet
Cover design & interior layout: Rachel Thern

NOUMENA  CLASSICS
THE CHILD IN THE HOUSE
and Other Imaginary Portraits
by Walter Pater

The Child in the House
In an idealized memory of childhood, a young boy's awareness
of the world around him blossoms—an awareness of beauty
and wonder, but also of death . . .

An English Poet
The meeting of a mysterious stranger and a fanciful young
woman results in the auspicious birth of a child with the soul
of a poet . . .

Emerald Uthwart
A submissive youth from a venerable family goes off to school
and befriends a kindred spirit, but when war breaks out the
two make a fateful decision that will forever change the course
of their lives . . .

Walter Horatio Pater (1839-1894) was an English essayist, art
critic, and academic best remembered for his *Studies in the
History of the Renaissance* (1873), a book at the forefront of the
Aesthetic Movement, which considered a successful life to
"burn always with this hard, gemlike flame."

Pater also wrote a series of what he termed "Imaginary
Portraits:" a type of literary vignette of his own devising
that masterfully blended elements of biography, prose
poem, and short story. While most of the Portraits take
the form of historical recreations, the three collected in this
edition are more contemporary to Pater's own time and are
perhaps the most autobiographical. Previously appearing
in the posthumous *Miscellaneous Studies* (1895), "The Child
in the House" and "Emerald Uthwart" are better served
thematically in a separate volume. They are reprinted here
along with a fragment entitled "An English Poet," a nearly
forgotten Imaginary Portrait which appears in book form for
the first time.

With regard to its influence, there is strong evidence to
suggest that "The Child in the House" was a major—or quite
possibly even indispensable—inspiration for Proust in his
writing of *In Search of Lost Time*.

Walter Pater

I wish to dedicate this edition to the memory of my father, Professor Gary D. Allinson (1942-2006), to whom I very much would have liked to present this little book.

RJA

Table of Contents

List of Plates

"An English Poet" made its first published appearance in the 1 April 1931 issue of The Fortnightly Review *with the following prefatory note. Since it mentions the three pieces included in this edition, it will serve nicely as an introduction to this particular collection of* Imaginary Portraits. *Its author, May Ottley, was a pupil of Pater's sister Clara and the wife of Robert Ottley, the Canon of Christ Church at Oxford.*

A few words of elaboration upon some of the references in Mrs. Ottley's introduction may be of use here:

Gaston de Latour (1896) *is an "unfinished romance" by Pater concerning the spiritual awakening of a young French nobleman in the 16th century; Dr. Johnson refers to the famous author of the* Dictionary of the English Language (1755).

"He who blows through bronze may breathe through silver" is a line from the 13th canto of Robert Browning's poem "One Word More" (1855).

In addition to the famous cathedral, Canterbury in Kent is also home to The King's School, which is said to have been founded by the Benedictine monk and first Archbishop of Canterbury, Augustine of Canterbury, in the late 6th century. It became known under its present name during the reign of Henry VIII when it was seized from Catholic control and rededicated to the king. By the time of Pater's attendance (1853-1858), the King's School had transitioned from being a traditional grammar school into a "public school:" a selective, private institution for young men, either as boarders or as day pupils.

Miscellaneous Studies (1895) *is a posthumous collection which, in addition to "The Child in the House" and "Emerald Uthwart" also includes the essays "Prosper Mérimée," "Raphael," "Pascal," "Art Notes in North Italy," "Notre-Dame d'Amiens," "Vézelay," "Apollo in Picardy," and "Diaphaneitè."*

The Prelude *is an autobiographical poem by Wordsworth, generally considered to be his finest work; the quote that follows it, as the reader will soon see, is from "The Child in the House;" "Of quality and fabric more divine" is the final line from "The Prelude."*

Charles Shadwell (1840-1919) was the provost of Oriel College, Oxford and Pater's literary executor; Sir Thomas Herbert Warren (1853-1930) was the President of Magdalen College, Oxford.

The "faultless painter" and the following stanza are references to another of Browning's poems entitled "Andrea del Sarto, Called 'the faultless painter'" (1855).

INTRODUCTION

When Mr. Pater died, in 1894, there was found among his papers a certain amount of fragmentary work, including a few incomplete chapters of *Gaston de Latour*, what promised to be a characteristically penetrating and illuminating study of Dr. Johnson, and an essay entitled *Imaginary Portraits. 2. An English Poet*. All these were written in his own exquisite handwriting in the manner peculiar to him, on quarto-size white or bluish-tinted paper with the carefully spaced lines, the blanks left here and there to be filled in, after laborious thought and search, with two, sometimes even three, possible words, from which, in the end, "le mot juste" was to be chosen; the closely-packed leaves, each one numbered, and so, page after page, finished at last, and tied together finally with a neat scrap of ribbon. From this meticulously careful and uniform method, Mr. Pater never seems to have deviated. It is a witness to the spirit of the artist to whom fidelity in detail meant what it means to the architect, or to the builder of a great ship; an inalienable and essential part of the perfected work. Those who knew Mr. Pater personally, or those who seem to see the reflection of his elusive, austere, high-souled character in what he wrote and the way in which he wrote, must needs be struck by the singular quality of the style and the man   the subtle blending of strength and beauty, of power and delicacy, of restraint and imagination, of the Puritan and the Platonist—which gives him an individual stamp and an individual place among great English prose writers. "He who blows through bronze may breathe through silver."

The title of the essay printed here is significant—*Imaginary Portrait, Number 2.* The first essay to be published under a similar heading was that most perfect autobiographical gem, *The Child in the House*, which appeared in *Macmillan's Magazine* in August, 1878. Closely associated with this is *Emerald Uthwart*, the noble and moving record of those far-off, unforgettable days and experiences of the writer's boyhood under the shadow of the Cathedral at Canterbury. It was written soon after Mr. Pater's last visit to his old school, in the summer of 1891, a visit which revivified fading memories, and evoked an eager response to the impressions of the moment. "The very place one is in, its stone-work, its empty spaces, invade you; invade all who belong to them, as Uthwart belongs, yielding wholly from the first." Or, later on, in allusion to the second character-building environment of his early life: "In truth, the memory of Oxford made almost everything he saw after it seem vulgar." Again—and indeed a short sentence seems to reveal the very heart of the essay, "the mere beauties of the place counted at the moment for less than in retrospect." *Emerald Uthwart* was published in 1892, in two consecutive numbers of the *New Review*. In his collected works both these essays are included in the volume entitled *Miscellaneous Studies*. Of the three, Mr. Pater himself gave the name *Imaginary Portrait* only to the *Child in the House* and to the hitherto unpublished *English Poet*, as if these two contained some deeper, more intimate self-revelation than does *Emerald Uthwart* even. And, in all three, as in the final script of the Prelude, the reader discerns the "finer sort of memory, bringing its object to mind with great clearness, yet, as sometimes happens in dreams, raised a little above itself and above ordinary retrospect."

Autobiography, of such sort, may lack what is commonly called veracity, but it has an added quality, an aroma of the past. It is indeed "of quality and fabric more divine."

After Mr. Pater's death, Dr. Shadwell and Sir Herbert Warren examined the few stray MSS., and rejected for publication, on the ground of their incompleteness, the unfinished chapters of *Gaston*, and, one imagines, the essay on Dr. Johnson, and *An English Poet*. It is true that a certain part of the unfinished *Gaston* was selected by them, and incorporated in the book as the reader knows it, but it was felt at the moment that all other fragmentary or uncompleted work should be left unpublished. But, as time passed, it became more and more clearly evident that this delicate, flexible prose was to find a lofty and permanent place in English literature. In the light of this fact it would seem an ill-judged surrender to conditions and opinions of thirty years' standing, to withhold from publication this early attempt to define, and reveal the growth of, those qualities which the reader of Mr. Pater associates with all his work. That it is the study of a young aspiring artist lends to its interest. Posterity has eagerly seized upon the immature or fragmentary work of poets and of painters, and has found even, as e.g., in Leonardo's study of St. Anne, a deeper significance and a deeper satisfaction than in his more finished work. The "faultless painter's" lament struck, and still strikes, the authentic note:

> Their works drop groundward, but themselves, I know
> Reach many a time a heaven that's shut to me;
> Enter and take their place there sure enough,
> Though they came back and cannot tell the world.

In this early essay, with its intimate self-revelation, the sympathetic reader is privileged to discern the latent characteristics which moulded Mr. Pater's unique style, a style so wholly personal and inimitable, a style so closely akin to poetry, yet, in its intellectuality, its reserve, its strength, exalted into such noble and splendid prose. The idea, running like a thread of gold through the whole essay—the blended imagery of the honeysuckle, in its frail and fleeting beauty of colour and scent, with the delicate power of the flower metal-screen work, haunting the growing boy like a passion, never to leave him in all his later years—how symbolic of the character and the work of the writer! All the superficial, stupid, cruel and crude misjudgments of those early years crumble into dust in the face of the halting sincerity of a young man, trying to reveal himself *to* himself, in this most intimate attempt.

"Afterwards, when he was understood to be a poet, this, a peculiar character as of flowers in metal, was noticed by the curious as a distinction in his verse, such an elastic force in word and phrase, following a delicate thought or feeling as the metal followed the curvature of the flower, as seemed to indicate an artistic triumph over a material partly resisting, which yet at last took outline from his thought with the firmness of antique forms of mastery."

The editor of the essay has touched it as little as is possible. Of a choice of words, that written last, or at the top of one or two others, is as a rule, printed here; defective words or phrases are marked by brackets or a question mark. Sometimes, in the original essay, the grammar is faulty, and therefore the sense is obscure. The editor has taken the liberty of cutting out one or two unessential passages. What is left would seem to be "of quality and fabric," such as no lover of Walter Pater would willingly let die.

[M.O.]

The Child in the House
August 1878

As Florian Deleal walked, one hot afternoon, he overtook by the wayside a poor aged man, and, as he seemed weary with the road, helped him on with the burden which he carried, a certain distance. And as the man told his story, it chanced that he named the place, a little place in the neighbourhood of a great city, where Florian had passed his earliest years, but which he had never since seen, and, the story told, went forward on his journey comforted. And that night, like a reward for his pity, a dream of that place came to Florian, a dream which did for him the office of the finer sort of memory, bringing its object to mind with a great clearness, yet, as sometimes happens in dreams, raised a little above itself, and above ordinary retrospect. The true aspect of the place, especially of the house there in which he had lived as a child, the fashion of its doors, its hearths, its windows, the very scent upon the air of it, was with him in sleep for a season; only, with tints more musically blent on wall and floor, and some finer light and shadow running in and out along its curves and angles, and with all its little carvings daintier. He awoke with a sigh at the thought of almost thirty years which lay between him and that place, yet with a flutter of pleasure still within him at the fair light, as if it were a smile, upon it. And it happened that this accident of his dream was just the thing needed for the beginning of a certain design he then had in view, the noting, namely, of some things in the story of his spirit—in that process of brain building by which we are, each one of

3

us, what we are. With the image of the place so clear and favourable upon him, he fell to thinking of himself therein, and how his thoughts had grown upon him. In that half-spiritualised house he could watch the better, over again, the gradual expansion of the soul which had come to be there—of which indeed, through the law which makes the material objects about them so large an element in children's lives, it had actually become a part; inward and outward being woven through and through each other into one inextricable texture—half, tint and trace and accident of homely colour and form, from the wood and the bricks of it; half, mere soul-stuff, floated thither from who knows how far. In the house and garden of his dream he saw a child moving, and could divide the main streams, at least, of the winds that had played on him, and study so the first stage in that mental journey.

The *old house*, as when Florian talked of it afterwards he always called it, (as all children do, who can recollect a change of home, soon enough but not too soon to mark a period in their lives) really was an old house; and an element of French descent in its inmates—descent from Watteau,* the old court-painter, one of whose gallant pieces still hung in one of the rooms—might explain, together with some other things, a noticeable trimness and comely whiteness about everything there—the curtains, the couches, the paint on the walls with which the light and shadow played so delicately, might explain also the tolerance of the great poplar in the garden, a tree most often despised by English people, but which French people love, having observed a certain fresh way its leaves have of dealing with the wind, making it sound, in never so light a stirring of the air, like running water.

The old-fashioned, low wainscoting went round the rooms, and up the staircase with carved balusters and shadowy angles, landing half-way up at a broad

4

window, with a swallow's nest below the sill, and the blossom of an old pear-tree showing across it in late April, against the blue, below which the perfumed juice of the find of fallen fruit in autumn was so fresh. At the next turning came the closet which held on its deep shelves the best china. Little angel faces, and reedy flutings stood out round the fireplace of the children's room. And on the top of the house, above the large attic, where the white mice ran in the twilight—an infinite, unexplored wonderland of childish treasures, glass beads, empty scent-bottles still sweet, thrum of coloured silks, among its lumber—a flat space of roof, railed about, gave a view of the neighbouring steeples; for the house, as I said, stood near a great city, which sent up heavenwards, over the twisting weather-vanes, not seldom, its beds of rolling cloud and smoke, touched with storm or sunshine. But the child of whom I am writing did not hate the fog for the crimson lights which fell from it sometimes upon the chimneys, and the whites which gleamed through its openings, on summer mornings, on turret or pavement. For it is false to suppose that a child's sense of beauty is dependent on any choiceness, or special fineness, in the objects which present themselves to it, though this indeed comes to be the rule with most of us in later life; earlier, in some degree, we see inwardly; and the child finds for itself, and with unstinted delight, a difference for the sense, in those whites and reds through the smoke on very homely buildings, and in the gold of the dandelions at the road-side, just beyond the houses, where not a handful of earth is virgin and untouched, in the lack of better ministries to its desire of beauty.

This house, then, stood not far beyond the gloom and rumours of the town, among high garden-walls, bright all summer-time with Golden-rod, and brown-and-golden Wall-flower,—*Flos Parietis*,* as the children's Latin-reading father taught them to call it, while he was

5

with them. Tracing back the threads of his complex spiritual habit, as he was used in after years to do, Florian found that he owed to the place many tones of sentiment afterwards customary with him, certain inward lights under which things most naturally presented themselves to him. The coming and going of travellers to the town along the way, the shadow of the streets, the sudden breadth of the neighbouring gardens, the singular brightness of bright weather there, its singular darknesses which linked themselves in his mind to certain engraved illustrations in the old big Bible at home, the coolness of the dark, cavernous shops round the great church, with its giddy winding stair up to the pigeons and the bells—a citadel of peace in the heart of the trouble—all this acted on his childish fancy, so that ever afterwards the like aspects and incidents never failed to throw him into a well-recognised imaginative mood, seeming actually to have become a part of the texture of his mind. Also, Florian could trace home to this point an all-pervading preference in himself for a kind of comeliness and dignity, an *urbanity* literally, in modes of life, which he connected with the pale people of towns, and which made him susceptible to a kind of exquisite satisfaction in the trimness and well-considered grace of certain things and persons he afterwards met with, here and there, in his way through the world.

So the child of whom I am writing lived on there quietly; things without thus ministering to him, as he sat daily at the window with the birdcage hanging below it, and his mother taught him to read, wondering at the ease with which he learned, and at the quickness of his memory. The perfume of the little flowers of the lime-tree fell through the air upon them, like rain; while time seemed to move ever more slowly to the murmur of the bees in it, till it almost stood still on June afternoons. How insignificant, at the moment, seem the influences of the sensible things which are tossed and fall and lie

6

about us, so, or so, in the environment of early child-hood. How indelibly, as we afterwards discover, they affect us; with what capricious attractions and associations they figure themselves on the white paper, the smooth wax of our ingenuous souls, as "with lead in the rock for ever,"* giving form and feature, and as it were assigned house-room in our memory, to early experiences of feeling and thought, which abide with us ever afterwards, thus, and not otherwise. The realities and passions, the rumours of the greater world without, steal in upon us, each by its own special little passage-way, through the wall of custom about us; and never afterwards quite detach themselves from this or that accident, or trick, in the mode of their first entrance to us. Our susceptibilities, the discovery of our powers, manifold experiences—our various experiences of the coming and going of bodily pain, for instance—belong to this or the other well-remembered place in the material habitation—that little white room with the window across which the heavy blossoms could beat so peevish-ly in the wind, with just that particular catch or throb, such a sense of teasing in it, on gusty mornings: and the early habitation thus gradually becomes a sort of material shrine or sanctuary of sentiment; a system of visible symbolism interweaves itself through all our thoughts and passions; and, irresistibly, little shapes, voices, accidents—the angle at which the sun in the morning fell on the pillow—become parts of the great chain wherewith we are bound.

Thus far, for Florian, what all this had determined was a peculiarly strong sense of home—so forcible a motive with all of us—prompting to us our customary love of the earth, and the larger part of our fear of death, that revulsion we have from it, as from something strange, untried, unfriendly; though life-long imprisonment, they tell you, and final banishment from home is a thing bitterer still; the looking forward to but a short space, a

7

mere childish *goûter** and dessert of it, before the end, being so great a resource of effort to pilgrims and wayfarers, and the soldier in distant quarters, and lending, in lack of that, some power of solace to the thought of sleep in the home churchyard at least, dead cheek by dead cheek, and with the rain soaking in upon one from above.

So powerful is this instinct, and yet such accidents as these so mechanically determine it; its essence being indeed the early familiar, as constituting our ideal, or typical conception, of rest and security. Out of so many possible conditions, just this for you, and that for me, brings ever the unmistakable realisation of the delightful *chez soi;** this for the Englishman, for me and you, with the closely-drawn white curtain and the shaded lamp; that, quite other, for the wandering Arab, who folds his tent every morning, and makes his sleeping place among haunted ruins, or in old tombs.

With Florian, then, the sense of home became singularly intense, his good fortune being that the special character of his home was in itself so essentially home-like. As, after many wanderings, I have come to fancy that some parts of Surrey and Kent are, for Englishmen, the true landscape, true home-counties, by right, partly, of a certain earthy warmth in the yellow of the sand below their gorse-bushes, and of a certain grey-blue mist after rain, in the hollows of the hills there, welcome to fatigued eyes, and never seen farther south; so I think that the sort of house I have described, with precisely those proportions of red-brick and green, and with a just perceptible monotony in the subdued order of it, for its distinguishing note, is, for Englishmen at least, typically home-like. And so for Florian that general human instinct was reinforced by this special home-likeness in the place the wandering soul of him had happened to light on, as, in the second degree, its body and earthly tabernacle; the sense of harmony between such soul and

8

its physical environment became, for a time at least, like perfectly played music, and the life led there singularly tranquil and filled with a curious sense of self-possession. The love of security, of an habitually undisputed standing-ground or sleeping-place, came to count for much in the generation and correcting of his thoughts, and afterwards as a salutary principle of restraint in all his wanderings of spirit. The wistful yearning towards home, in absence from it, as the shadows of evening deepened, and he followed in thought what was doing there from hour to hour, interpreted to him much of a yearning and regret he experienced afterwards, towards he knew not what, out of strange ways of feeling and thought in which, from time to time, his spirit found itself alone; and in the tears shed in such absences there seemed always to be some soul-subduing foretaste of what his last tears might be.

So the sense of security could hardly have been deeper, the quiet of the child's soul being one with the quiet of its home, a place "inclosed" and "sealed." But upon this assured place, upon the child's assured soul, which resembled it, there came floating in from the larger world without, as at windows left ajar unknowingly, or over the high garden walls, two streams of impressions, the sentiments of beauty and pain—recognitions of the visible, tangible, audible loveliness of things, as a very real and somewhat tyrannous element in them— and of the sorrow of the world, of grown people, and children and animals, as a thing not to be put by in them. From this point he could trace two predominant processes of mental change in him—the growth of an almost diseased sensibility to the spectacle of suffering, and, parallel with this, the surprisingly rapid growth of a certain capacity of fascination by bright colour and choice form—the sweet curvings, for instance, of the lips of those who seemed to him comely persons, modulated in such delicate unison to the things they said

9

or sang—marking early the activity in him of a more than customary sensuousness, "the lust of the eye,"* as the Preacher says, which might lead him, one day, how far! Could he have foreseen the weariness of the way! In music sometimes the two sorts of impressions came together, and he would weep, to the surprise of older people. Tears of joy, too, the child knew, also to older people's surprise; real tears, once, of relief from long-strung, childish expectation, when he found returned at evening, with new roses in her cheeks, the little sister who had been to a place where there was a wood, and brought back for him a treasure of fallen acorns, and black crow's feathers, and the peace at finding her again near him mingled all night with some intimate sense in him of the distant forest, the rumour of its breezes, with the glossy blackbirds aslant and the branches lifted in them, and of the perfect nicety of the little cups that fell. So those two elementary apprehensions of the tenderness and of the colour in things grew apace in him, and were seen by him afterwards to send their roots back into the beginnings of life.

Let me note first some of the occasions of his recognition of the element of pain in things—incidents, now and again, which seemed suddenly to awake in him the whole force of that sentiment which Goethe has called the *Weltschmerz*, and in which the concentrated sorrow of the world seemed suddenly to lie heavy upon him. A book lay in an old book-case, of which he cared to remember one picture—a woman sitting with hands bound behind her, the dress, the cap, the hair, folded with a simplicity which touched him strangely, as if not by her own hands, but with some ambiguous care at the hands of others—Queen Marie Antoinette, on her way to execution—we all remember David's drawing,* meant merely to make her ridiculous. The face that had been so high had learned to be mute and resistless; but out of its very resistlessness, seemed now to call on men

10

to have pity, and forbear; and he took note of that, as he closed the book, as a thing to look at again, if he should at any time find himself tempted to be cruel. Again, he would never quite forget the appeal in the small sister's face, in the garden under the lilacs, terrified at a spider lighted on her sleeve. He could trace back to the look then noted a certain mercy he conceived always for people in fear, even of little things, which seemed to make him, though but for a moment, capable of almost any sacrifice of himself. Impressible, susceptible persons, indeed, who had had their sorrows, lived about him; and this sensibility was due in part to the tacit influence of their presence, enforcing upon him habitually the fact that there are those who pass their days, as a matter of course, in a sort of "going quietly." Most poignantly of all he could recall, in unfading minutest circumstance, the cry on the stair, sounding bitterly through the house, and struck into his soul for ever, of an aged woman, his father's sister, come now to announce his death in distant India; how it seemed to make the aged woman like a child again; and, he knew not why, but this fancy was full of pity to him. There were the little sorrows of the dumb animals too—of the white angora, with a dark tail like an ermine's, and a face like a flower, who fell into a lingering sickness, and became quite delicately human in its valetudinarianism, and came to have a hundred different expressions of voice—how it grew worse and worse, till it began to feel the light too much for it, and at last, after one wild morning of pain, the little soul flickered away from the body, quite worn to death already, and now but feebly retaining it.

So he wanted another pet; and as there were starlings about the place, which could be taught to speak, one of them was caught, and he meant to treat it kindly: but in the night its young ones could be heard crying after it, and the responsive cry of the mother-bird towards

11

them; and at last, with the first light, though not till after some debate with himself, he went down and opened the cage, and saw a sharp bound of the prisoner up to her nestlings; and therewith came the sense of remorse, that he too was become an accomplice in moving, to the limit of his small power, the springs and handles of that great machine in things, constructed so ingeniously to play pain-fugues on the delicate nerve-work of living creatures.

I have remarked how, in the process of our brain-building, as the house of thought in which we live gets itself together, like some airy bird's nest of floating thistle-down and chance straws, compact at last, little accidents have their consequence; and thus it happened that, as he walked one evening, a garden gate, usually closed, stood open; and lo! within, a great red hawthorn, in full flower, embossing heavily the bleached and twisted trunk and branches, so aged that there were but few green leaves thereon—a plumage of tender, crimson fire out of the heart of the dry wood. The perfume of the tree had now and again reached him, in the currents of the wind, over the wall, and he had wondered what might be behind it, and was now allowed to fill his arms with the flowers—flowers enough for all the old blue-china pots along the chimney-piece, making *fête* in the children's room. Was it some periodic moment in the expansion of soul within him, or mere trick of heat in the heavily-laden summer air? But the beauty of the thing struck home to him feverishly, and in dreams, all night, he loitered along a magic roadway of crimson flowers, which seemed to open ruddily in thick, fresh masses about his feet, and fill softly all the little hollows in the banks on either side. Always afterwards, summer by summer, as the flowers came on, the blossom of the red hawthorn still seemed to him absolutely the reddest of all things; and the goodly crimson, still alive in the works of old Venetian masters, or old

12

Flemish tapestries, called out always from afar, the recollection of the flame in those perishing little petals, as it pulsed gradually out of them, kept long in the drawers of an old cabinet. Also then, for the first time, he seemed to experience a passionateness in his relation to fair outward objects, an inexplicable excitement in their presence, which disturbed him, and from which he half longed to be free. A touch of regret or desire mingled all night with the remembered presence of the red flowers, and their perfume in the darkness about him; and the longing for some undivined, entire possession of them was the beginning of a revelation to him, growing ever clearer, with the coming of the gracious summer guise of fields, and trees, and persons in each succeeding year, of a certain, at times seemingly exclusive, predominance in his interests of beautiful physical things, a kind of tyranny of the senses over him.

In later years he came upon philosophies which occupied him much in the estimate of the proportion of the sensuous and the ideal elements in human knowledge, the relative parts they bear in it; and, in his intellectual scheme, was led to assign very little to the abstract thought, and much to its sensible vehicle or occasion. Such metaphysical speculation did but reinforce what was instinctive in his way of receiving the world, and for him, everywhere, that sensible vehicle or occasion became, perhaps only too surely, the necessary concomitant of any perception of things, real enough to be of any weight or reckoning, in his house of thought. There were times when he could think of the necessity he was under of associating all thoughts to touch and sight, as a sympathetic link between himself and actual, feeling, living objects; a protest in favour of real men and women against mere grey, unreal abstractions; and he remembered gratefully how the Christian religion, hardly less than the religion of the ancient Greeks, translating so much of its spiritual verily into things that may

13

be seen, condescends in part to sanction this infirmity, if so it be, of our human existence, wherein the world of sense is so much with us, and welcomed this thought as a kind of keeper and sentinel over his soul therein. But, certainly he came, more and more, to be unable to care for, or think of soul but as in an actual body, or of any world but that wherein are water and trees, and where men and women look, so or so, and press actual hands. It was the trick even his pity learned, fastening those who suffered in anywise to his affections by a kind of sensible attachments. He would think of Julian, fallen into incurable sickness, as spoiled in the sweet blossom of his skin like pale amber, and his honey-like hair; of Cecil, early dead, as cut off from the lilies, from golden summer days, from women's voices; and then what comforted him a little was the thought of the turning of the child's flesh to violets in the turf above him. And thinking of the very poor, it was not the things which most men care most for that he yearned to give them; but fairer roses, perhaps, and power to taste quite as they will, at their ease and not task-burdened, a certain desirable, clear light in the new morning, through which sometimes he had noticed them, quite unconscious of it, on their way to their early toil.

So he yielded himself to these things, to be played upon by them like a musical instrument, and began to note with deepening watchfulness, but always with some puzzled, unutterable longing in his enjoyment, the phases of the seasons and of the growing or waning day, down even to the shadowy changes wrought on bare wall or ceiling—the light cast up from the snow, bringing out their darkest angles; the brown light in the cloud, which meant rain; that almost too austere clearness, in the protracted light of the lengthening day, before warm weather began, as if it lingered but to make a severer workday, with the school-books opened earlier and later; that beam of June sunshine, at last, as he lay awake before the time, a way of gold-dust across the darkness; all the humming, the freshness, the perfume of the garden seemed to lie upon it—and coming in one afternoon in September, along the red gravel walk, to look for a basket of yellow crab-apples left in the cool, old parlour, he remembered it the more, and how the colours struck upon him, because a wasp on one bitten apple stung him, and he felt the passion of sudden, severe pain. For this too brought its curious reflexions; and, in relief from it, he would wonder over it—how it had then been with him—puzzled at the depth of the charm or spell over him, which lay, for a little while at least, in the mere absence of pain; once, especially, when an older boy taught him to make flowers of sealing-wax, and he had burnt his hand badly at the lighted taper, and been unable to sleep. He remembered that also afterwards, as a sort of typical thing—a white vision of heat about him, clinging closely, through the languid scent of the ointments put upon the place to make it well.

Also, as he felt this pressure upon him of the sensible world, then, as often afterwards, there would come another sort of curious questioning how the last impressions of eye and ear might happen to him, how they would find him—the scent of the last flower, the soft yellowness of the last morning, the last recognition of some object of affection, hand or voice; it could not be but that the latest look of the eyes, before their final closing, would be strangely vivid; one would go with the hot tears, the cry, the touch of the wistful bystander, impressed how deeply on one! or would it be, perhaps, a mere frail retiring of all things, great or little, away from one, into a level distance?

For with this desire of physical beauty mingled itself early the fear of death—the fear of death intensified by the desire of beauty. Hitherto he had never gazed upon dead faces, as sometimes, afterwards, at the *Morgue* in Paris,* or in that fair cemetery at Munich, where all the

15

dead must go and lie in state before burial, behind glass windows, among the flowers and incense and holy candles—the aged clergy with their sacred ornaments, the young men in their dancing-shoes and spotless white linen—after which visits, those waxen, resistless faces would always live with him for many days, making the broadest sunshine sickly. The child had heard indeed of the death of his father, and how, in the Indian station, a fever had taken him, so that though not in action he had yet died as a soldier; and hearing of the "resurrection of the just," he could think of him as still abroad in the world, somehow, for his protection—a grand, though perhaps rather terrible figure, in beautiful soldier's things, like the figure in the picture of Joshua's Vision in the Bible*—and of that, round which the mourners moved so softly, and afterwards with such solemn singing, as but a worn-out garment left at a deserted lodging. So it was, until on a summer day he walked with his mother through a fair churchyard. In a bright dress he rambled among the graves, in the gay weather, and so came, in one corner, upon an open grave for a child—a dark space on the brilliant grass—the black mould lying heaped up round it, weighing down the little jewelled branches of the dwarf rose-bushes in flower. And therewith came, full-grown, never wholly to leave him, with the certainty that even children do sometimes die, the physical horror of death, with its wholly selfish recoil from the association of lower forms of life, and the suffocating weight above. No benign, grave figure in beautiful soldier's things any longer abroad in the world for his protection! only a few poor, piteous bones; and above them, possibly, a certain sort of figure he hoped not to see. For sitting one day in the garden below an open window, he heard people talking, and could not but listen, how, in a sleepless hour, a sick woman had seen one of the dead sitting beside her, come to call her hence; and from the broken talk, evolved with much

16

clearness the notion that not all those dead people had really departed to the churchyard, nor were quite so motionless as they looked, but led a secret, half-fugitive life in their old homes, quite free by night, though sometimes visible in the day, dodging from room to room, with no great goodwill towards those who shared the place with them. All night the figure sat beside him in the reveries of his broken sleep, and was not quite gone in the morning—an odd, irreconcilable new member of the household, making the sweet familiar chambers unfriendly and suspect by its uncertain presence. He could have hated the dead he had pitied so, for being thus. Afterwards he came to think of those poor, home-returning ghosts, which all men have fancied to themselves—the *revenants*—pathetically, as crying, or beating with vain hands at the doors, as the wind came, their cries distinguishable in it as a wilder inner note. But, always making death more unfamiliar still, that old experience would ever, from time to time, return to him; even in the living he sometimes caught its likeness; at any time or place, in a moment, the faint atmosphere of the chamber of death would be breathed around him, and the image with the bound chin, the quaint smile, the straight, stiff feet, shed itself across the air upon the bright carpet, amid the gayest company, or happiest communing with himself.

To most children the sombre questionings to which impressions like these attach themselves, if they come at all, are actually suggested by religious books, which therefore they often regard with much secret distaste, and dismiss, as far as possible, from their habitual thoughts as a too depressing element in life. To Florian such impressions, these misgivings as to the ultimate tendency of the years, of the relationship between life and death, had been suggested spontaneously in the natural course of his mental growth by a strong innate sense for the soberer tones in things, further

17

strengthened by actual circumstances; and religious sentiment, that system of biblical ideas in which he had been brought up, presented itself to him as a thing that might soften and dignify, and light up as with a "lively hope,"* a melancholy already deeply settled in him. So he yielded himself easily to religious impressions, and with a kind of mystical appetite for sacred things; the more as they came to him through a saintly person who loved him tenderly, and believed that this early pre-occupation with them already marked the child out for a saint. He began to love, for their own sakes, church lights, holy days, all that belonged to the comely order of the sanctuary, the secrets of its white linen, and holy vessels, and fonts of pure water; and its hieratic purity and simplicity became the type of something he desired always to have about him in actual life. He pored over the pictures in religious books, and knew by heart the exact mode in which the wrestling angel grasped Jacob, how Jacob looked in his mysterious sleep, how the bells and pomegranates were attached to the hem of Aaron's vestment,* sounding sweetly as he glided over the turf of the holy place. His way of conceiving religion came then to be in effect what it ever afterwards remained—a sacred history, indeed, but still more a sacred ideal, a transcendent version or representation, under intenser and more expressive light and shade, of human life and its familiar or exceptional incidents, birth, death, marriage, youth, age, tears, joy, rest, sleep, waking—a mirror, towards which men might turn away their eyes from vanity and dullness, and see themselves therein as angels, with their daily meat and drink, even, become a kind of sacred transaction—a complementary strain or burden, applied to our every-day existence, whereby the stray snatches of music in it re-set themselves, and fall into the scheme of some higher and more consistent harmony. A place adumbrated itself in his thoughts, wherein those sacred personalities, which are at once

18

the reflex and the pattern of our nobler phases of life, housed themselves; and this region in his intellectual scheme all subsequent experience did but tend still further to realise and define. Some ideal, hieratic persons he would always need to occupy it and keep a warmth there. And he could hardly understand those who felt no such need at all, finding themselves quite happy without such heavenly companionship, and sacred double of their life, beside them.

Thus a constant substitution of the typical for the actual took place in his thoughts. Angels might be met by the way, under English elm or beech-tree; mere messengers seemed like angels, bound on celestial errands; a deep mysticity brooded over real meetings and partings; marriages were made in heaven; and deaths also, with hands of angels thereupon, to bear soul and body quietly asunder, each to its appointed rest. All the acts and accidents of daily life borrowed a sacred colour and significance; the very colours of things became themselves weighty with meanings like the sacred stuffs of Moses' tabernacle, full of penitence or peace. Sentiment, congruous in the first instance only with those divine transactions, the deep, effusive unction of the House of Bethany,* was assumed as the due attitude for the reception of our every-day existence; and for a time he walked through the world in a sustained, not unpleasurable awe, generated by the habitual recognition, beside every circumstance and event of life, of its celestial correspondent.

Sensibility—the desire of physical beauty—a strange biblical awe, which made any reference to the unseen act on him like solemn music—these qualities the child took away with him, when, at about the age of twelve years, he left the old house, and was taken to live in another place. He had never left home before, and, anticipating much from this change, had long dreamed over it, jealously counting the days till the time fixed for departure should come: had been a little careless about others, even, in his strong desire for it—when Lewis fell sick, for instance, and they must wait still two days longer. At last the morning came, very fine; and all things—the very pavement with its dust, at the road-side—seemed to have a white, pearl-like lustre in them. They were to travel by a favourite road on which he had often walked a certain distance, and on one of those two prisoner days, when Lewis was sick, had walked farther than ever before, in his great desire to reach the new place. They had started and gone a little way when a pet bird was found to have been left behind, and must even now—so it presented itself to him—have already all the appealing fierceness and wild self-pity at heart of one left by others to perish of hunger in a closed house; and he returned to fetch it, himself in hardly less stormy distress. But as he passed in search of it from room to room, lying so pale, with a look of meekness in their denudation, and at last through that little, stripped white room, the aspect of the place touched him like the face of one dead; and a clinging back towards it came over him, so intense that he knew it would last long, and spoiling all his pleasure in the realisation of a thing so eagerly anticipated. And so, with the bird found, but himself in an agony of home-sickness, thus capriciously sprung up within him, he was driven quickly away, far into the rural distance, so fondly speculated on, of that favourite country-road.

An English Poet
c. 1878

The great characteristic of the *Pays de Caux*,* the district from which our Norman conquerors mostly came, is the singular arrangement by which each of its farms is isolated from the outer world by a dense enclosure of trees. These square enclosures are dotted all over the high country, otherwise treeless—a broad expanse of corn declining to the edge of the white cliffs. On the sea-side of the enclosure the trees grow leaning from the salt wind—a smooth sloping wall of little rusty knots and twigs, the long bands of grey lichen growing thickly over them and keeping up in winter a faint semblance of foliage. The gate is usually surmounted by a rough pent-house, overgrown with moss and tall house-leeks, and the heavy stone gate-posts will be sometimes quaintly carved. In the space within there is room and to spare for the large straggling barns and the house with its white plastered walls. There is room for a garden also, and a careless orchard, where the blossoms hang almost motionless all their season through, although a strong wind may be abroad without, rocking roughly the bigger trees. The apples will be full of goodly juices, for the salt comes but faintly to them. Here the principle of the *chez-soi** is complete; in winter especially when the snow lies in deep drifts around the place, one has time for fancies, and the English girl, married to the plain young Norman farmer, who found in the furrow one autumn morning a golden Roman coin with a clear high profile on it which looked to her as might an image of immortal youth, is left alone with her day-dreams.

23

She showed the thing to the Curé, who told her how in the old Pagan times the darkened minds of men had been wont to think much more of the perishable beauty of the body than Christians are allowed to do.

And about that time when the little *bath* down below at the mouth of a tiny river, where the great ship came in, level with the rim of the cliffs, was filled with visitors from Paris, a bright figure came one afternoon when there were a thousand dancing shadows on the grass, and leaned upon the gate, a slim figure with delicate hands and golden hair growing crisply half down his forehead, and just such a profile as that on the golden medal. He has too, what the medal has not, colour— white and pale red, and just a touch of amber where the salt air of the channel has taken him. He leaned on the gate and asked her for one of the red apples which were lying in the grass and talked to her and laughed as he pressed his little white teeth through the crisp fruit. His mother is a great lady in Paris; nevertheless he finds it pleasant to talk with the pale English girl at the Norman farm, and he came and leaned on the gate again another afternoon.

Then the charmed, still autumn weather was suddenly broken up with a great rain; the wild Carrara mountains of cloud rose in a long line, passing slowly to the North-East, and all the visitors forsook the *bath* hastily, and went back to Paris.

Then all through that winter her heart was gently aflame, so that she conceived many quaint sentimentalities which to the eye of a poet might have revealed the delicate spirit which lay within her. Coming upon her stillness and isolation, the train of fancies which hung about the golden medal put a strange tincture of refinement upon all her daily habits. She sheltered the budding rose bush in its pot near the chimney corner and began to fancy that such things as flowers really felt neglect even, and pined over their own short lives, and

24

a little heart seemed breaking in each leaf that glided golden from the trees. So the rose bush was blossoming there in the red light on Christmas Day. But as the year's warmth came again and the sun penetrating the trees of the court threw again a legion of little dancing shadows up the white wall of her chamber where she kept the miniature of her dead mother above a posy of wild flowers, corn-cockles and yellow daisies, in a grey jar brought from Rouen fair, the fire in her heart was burning strong and wild and the light fancies were no longer at her will.

The bright figure with the low forehead never came to lean on the gate again, and the next winter she had in all the world nothing but the ashes of her fire, and the medal with the old Pagan face. I seem to see her taking still languidly those little household pleasures possible for those who are really stricken at heart underneath, with an expression I have sometimes seen on the faces of persons of very humble lot looking out on the world with a sort of wistfulness, in half conscious weariness of a life-task below their ideas and longing for a different one they can so easily imagine! yet quiet and modest withal, and faithful in affection to the plain young Frenchman she had married so young and to whose child, a fragile creature, she presently gave what remained of her own life.

That was the poet's mother. The languid child went early away to be reared in the braver air of its English relations among the stern Cumberland mountains.

When the traveller visits some celebrated spot among the mountains, Swiss or English even, to admire the deep lake or the precipice with its rose at twilight, doubly celebrated perhaps just now for the gallant adventure which ended in loss of life there a month before,* there is sometimes in his coming thus for mere amusement, did we but truly realise it, a contrast pathetic enough. For in these scenes, however beautiful, there are, over and above, those absolutely suffering, under whose windows we pass so ignorantly, waiting there so longingly for the reliever who comes not, those who in the full possession of their powers are in some sense bondmen there, those for whom the beautiful restful valley is but the barrier which shuts them from a possible happier field they know or dream of for the exercise of gifts felt slumbering within them. The solemn girdle of hills which seem to raise our jaded thoughts to themselves for a moment, does but shut them off from opportunity, from the city, the university, the brave gathering place of art, where the business of the mind is done, and the sacred fire is kept up whence *their* minds also might take sacred fire.

There are a certain number every year from whom these deep clefts of human life, prompted by mere commonplace or vulgar needs, break out for their *Wanderjahr*, to try their fortunes for better or worse in different places, returning home sometimes at the last, or lost oftener, as a large number of all migratory flocks never return. But one's pity is rather with that smaller number who with fully conscious desire for it never succeed in breaking out on their spiritual *Wanderjahr*. I never visit these places—places which the traveller only visits in summer, shuddering even then sometimes at the real chilliness there, so unproportioned to the shower which caused it—without meeting as I fancy, some of those who have been thus compelled to remain, to become consciously the mere material of a hard mechanical existence unsuited to them, and wonder that this impression does not often repress for people the pleasure of coming thither with a chill greater than that physical one. It is like visiting some place of exile or punishment, so alien yet so intimate, where the sensitive eyes now and then gaze at you as you pass along the graceless street, lingering into it for a few moments out of that forbidden garden where life is gayer, the inhabitants of which are yet so much more numerous than those, say, of Hallstadt,* or [   ] where the children's only treat is to eat sometimes the little white loaves of ordinary people's tables.

At such a place in Cumberland, a little town in one of its sterner districts, there was a boy, who felt, the whole year's experience being reckoned up, little but its physical hardness. He was the child of the consumptive girl who died amid such strange yearnings of heart at that Norman farm. And the rose after sunset, strangers looked up for so enthusiastically to the line of highest rocks above the fells, for him did but leave them more of the colour of ashes than before. The water-fall which chose to plunge down just into the middle of the town where the dwellings lay closest together, clinging grotesquely like pine trees to the steep mountain side, and which was as the chief accent of the place in the visitors' memory, was for the inhabitants useful indeed to grind the corn for their coarse bread, but from boy's point of view estimable only as for six days out of seven so much roughening of the air which set so sharply along the sunless streets; while he found the lake itself as it was perhaps always, a little wanting in celestial blueness. He felt with the vicissitudes of the whole year's round of the place upon him, the really dominant note of mere inclemency in a scenery supposed by summer visitors simply grand; and all through one exceptionally fine season which had brought thither more than the usual number of visitors, two things only of it all had coaxed out his capacity for liking—a red honey-suckle over the gateway of the grange, the one more stately habitation in the place, in remarkably free flower this year, and a range of metal screen-work, twisted with fantastic grace into wreaths of flames or flowers, noticed now for the first time, making fine shadows in the pale sunlight on the mellow whitewashed wall of the old church as he sat there on Sundays, himself except that thing, the one

27

touch of delicacy in its rudeness, and which seemed to him to hold somehow of that honey-suckle in flower and belong with it to a warmer heaven.

The honeysuckle was an exotic from France, the colour of its flower ripening from a peerless white to brown gold, with a whole round of fragrant changes in the spirit of the tiny thing still fragrant in death. And that ancient metal hand-work with its dainty traces of half-vanished gilding, an exotic that too from Augsburg where such metal flowers and flames are plenteous, really was a precious work of art, so that people of taste, though the boy did not know that, came from distant places to inspect it, and the pleasure in him at the fineness of a thing like that which made him think sometimes that *he* would be an artist in metal and be relieved of his dark heat of fancy in metal flower-work, marked already clearly enough his instinctive gift for the recognition of the seal of a master's hand. Afterwards, when he was understood to be a poet, this, a peculiar character as of flowers in metal, was noticed by the curious as a distinction in his verse, such an elastic force in word and phrase, following a tender delicate thought or feeling as the metal followed the curvature of the flower, as seemed to indicate artistic triumph over a material partly resisting, which yet at last took outline from his thought with the firmness of antique forms of mastery.

Those two slight things, then, the French honeysuckle and its image in the old German's forge-work, had met half-way a certain graciousness in his nature, the happier complement or reverse of that peevishness which the reader does not fail to see and may think a mere ague of the mind in him.

And a time came when the sense of certain gracious things not exotic, neglected in that early mountain abode, its morsels of more delicate texture, the native beauty of things that respond happily enough there to that severe northern air, such as the harebell and the heath, came to him freshly as if then first seen, and with a great reaching out of appetite towards them out of a feverish southern land, all the softer elements of that life at the lake side detached themselves from his memory and hung like a mirage over an imagined place he would fain have been in. For there *were* things, a delicate beauty about the Cumberland farm the boy never looked at; the tender plumage of the water-birds' breasts, for instance, against the dark lake as they went in squadron down it, leaving the long curves as if drawn with some fine artist's pen on the still surface at evening. He might have been thawed at least by the scent of the wood-lilies in spring, the scent of the free-flowing winds even at sunset, by the old immemorial poetry of the murmur of innumerable bees. But he valued none of these things.

A dim brooding divination of a great far-off world, the focus of all power and passion, where all precious things might well be plenteous, "the world," as we say, but as divined in ideal mood by the fine unprostituted soul of poetic youth, already possessed him. Those impassable mountains reinforcing the barrier of his birth as he thought, did but stimulate by limitation the imaginative sense of it. Beyond them flowed the tide of real existence, great affairs and great creations. Just so definite and no more was his sense of it! As yet he hardly connected it even with the life of great cities, and what the boy needed was rather fitting stimulus for the senses, some concrete imagery which might fix the wandering vision, that visible garment of which he saw not so much as the hem, means of expression or translation through which that dim brooding infinite sense, imaginativeness, might take hold, and he be relieved of the stifling weight of it. Only with his peculiar temper, chilled, repressed a little as with partly-suspended animation, it was necessary that such imagery should be exotic, that it should come with some secret of excitement, stirring him deftly from without.

And so it was only by pity sometimes he could check his distaste for the hard things mostly about him.

And one other object there was which had fixed his wandering gaze with a care for the visible beauty of it, afterwards powerfully superseded by that instinct of pity; the golden heads of two twin creatures almost never apart, in one common life of smiles, at the window in the thatch, on the door-step, under the elder-bushes. But they died early, chilled through by the dripping air of the mountain side, and touched him with a poignant sense of responsibility in love towards the house which became so still as they went to their tiny graves, leaving him alone with the benign, homely, silent woman who had made herself as his mother. That special appreciation of the maternal character which seems to cling to all creatures taken early from the breast, with a sort of unsatisfied yearning all their lives long, expanded in his poetic sense till he recognised its magnetic sweetness even in animal life, with a strange awe, and could fancy on the faces of ruddy school-boys the pressure of their mother's kisses, and between their lips the milk teeth still. A deep sense of warmth and rest at mind in the plain home burnt strong as at a red hearth in him, correcting what there was of selfishness in that longing for an exquisite and refined existence. And that odd yearning for the maternal character was as it were the more spiritual equivalent in this child so early taken from the breast, of the other merely sensuous longing for that warmer soil out of which exotic flowers or flowers of metal would naturally grow.

So it was with some leave takings, and with the sense of something torn within, as the boat drew away from the lake-side, that he departed at last to school. But here, in the quiet of holiday afternoons, in the westward light of the long windows of the bare whitewashed room or in golden hours next morning before waking time, a passion for reading came to him; and he found the exotic full-blown at last in books of prose and poetry. A sleepless, ever-shifting curiosity drove him far, hither and thither, to and fro, through the world of imaginative literature or what might stimulate imagination; the scarcely credible passages of science or travel or old life of kings and courtiers—often by devious ways and to points of view sometimes far remote from general reading. But a virile critical power summoning successive ideas of these impressions was awake too, and with a canon already very distinctly ascertained, of the measures and values to him of matters in the literary order. Coming to literature from so meagre a world, an actual world so meagre and grey, and depending on it for the satisfaction of his entire nature, of his very keenly awakened senses along with the rest of it, he must hold as his theory of the valuation of the products of art, that unless it were in some sort a revelation real as heat and cold, a discovery of hidden or distant things desirable to see, it was for him practically nowhere. The good book would be like an actual place visited, and to which one might return again and again at discretion for the infallible exercise therein of a special recognised influence, a certain controlling atmosphere, always to be experienced there, when one had a will to turn the key, acting almost independently of effort on one's own part, and remaining as an objective material fact while the pilgrim shifts to and fro. The shore with its tang of salt air, the house where you are to hear such or such songs, see such pictures, meet such people, or that great temple to which the sick came from afar to sleep, sure that a sacred dream would come to reveal how the sickness might be healed and with no fee due to the priests from the poor boy for letting him lie there; the genuine literary creations of past time have been not less palpable in influence; and a true education mainly consists in the well-pondered experience of what we shall find on demand in these places.

31

A series of such charmed places in literature the boy discovered and mapped out for himself [.]

There was this mood which with the desire of literary form, the ideal of literary life—became a motive high enough to purge out of an ambitious youth all that was common or unclean, and prompted an ideal so high that once to have conceived it, "il suffit que la pensée vous en soit venue pour que ma vie en demeure consolée et charmée."* There was the novelist with whom one lived in delicately haunted old New England mansions and Tuscan castles, country houses, yet far above the real America, or Italy, Apennine Tuscany even. There was one master of imaginative prose who might seem to bear on his single shoulders the whole Alpine world with no detail missing from root to crest, another raised a Valhalla of wild romantic architecture in which the heroes of all time sat together at last at their bitter heady wine. There was a poet through whom the expression of being "in the spirit" seemed clearly explained as he bore one deep into the Campagna of Rome or along the tender French coast; another whose English birds' song was sweet alike over lawn and fen-land; another whose reflections were like lonely chapels piled out of the ruins of holy places older still; another whose sacristy was a rich one—full—like the treasury of St. Mark's, of golden ornaments and *incense of Palestine.**

But it was not in lively-coloured modern books only that he was exercised; the intellectual hunger drew him freely into older English literature of many periods, and still always with a savour before all things of the style— how things were said—of manner—those elements of taste or of literary production which, because they are so delicately and individually apprehended and are yet so real, resemble physical sensations and may rightly be said to be the matter of a literary sense. Browne, Webster, Chapman* he discovered for himself on the neglected bookshelves and made his own anthology

32

from them. For him in these retrospective studies, as in all true appreciation of objects of art, the manner was the matter. What was strange was that, although half of foreign birth, he had come to be so sensitive of the resources of the English language, its rich expressiveness, its variety of cadence (the language of " ") with all the variety of that soft modulation at which foreigners with an ear wonder and admire. Expression, it may be verbal expression, holds of what may be called the feminine element and tradition in things, and is one of those elemental capacities which the child takes for the most part from its mother.

And such inheritance of an instinctive capacity for utterance he, the boy, had developed among the racy source of fully male English speech among the Cumberland mountains, and among people to whom a great English poet* attributed a certain natural superiority in the use of words.

And so it happened that while he hardly felt at all the impress of that same rich temperance in English scenery and English character, the English tongue had revealed itself to him as a living spirit of mysterious strength and sweetness and he had elected to be an artist in that. Out of the greyness and austerity of a school in which the senses pined while the fancy declined fondly towards a more exquisite mode of living, the boy required from words, and not in vain, in books, the picture, the tuberose, the marble face, the fading light on ancient cities, all that was not actually there for ear and eye, above all the genius of refinement; and this not as the new subject of writing, its more obvious and immediate presentations, but by a subtler operation from the style, the ether-like manner of the thing. So written language came to be form and colour as well as sound to him, exotic perfume almost. Having nothing else to live on, he extracted all they could yield from words, and his sense of them came to be curiously cultivated at all points.

"Words, words, words!" cries Hamlet,* stamping as he thinks all things with the very symbol of nothingness. To this poetic nature, sick like Hamlet, in a world partly "out of joint,"* words by themselves win not indeed more than daily food, yet sufficient to satisfy the cravings of that appetite in him which lives not by bread alone.

In the acquisition of this imaginative matter, and the cultivation of this delicate verbal cunning, his manner of proceeding was very sober and hard, as of one bent seriously on a task. There was even a kind of intellectual voluptuousness in that straining after means of sensation in books, kept up with so much of unfaltering purpose through so many years of strenuous youth, something of that physical greed you might trace in the extremely full lip and nostril, below the expectant, lifted, ethereal eyes and brow, feeding yet in the early day on the language of books, but expanding perhaps hereafter into quite other forms of appetite. And the manner of this hard firm-set diligence [   ] was smiled on kindly by a companion, the influence of whose gentle nature was yet towards the correction of what was hard or selfish in it. This friend was his confidant in many things, above all the boy's poetry. For in himself too gradually out of intent pondering over the work of others, the power of choice utterance was felt coming; and in those scraps of writing which the boyish poet shaped so well, so nearly perfectly, the friend found in turn the excitement, the stimulus, the fining influence of flight into new dainty places which the young poet had experienced in books.

For the strange boy himself there was a curious sense of relief in seeing thought or fancy, housed at last in the fragment of writing compressed, truly by many shapings, to some delightful inward pattern or ideal, which yet had weighed on him like a burden; for if your words regarding it are to be fragrant, he would say, you must have been for a time in slavish possession of the flower. It was a great pleasure, however pallid and intellectual, to have the literary morsel lying among the books, though for the eyes of one reader only, like a woman's ornament or a child's toy or a sea-shell lying safe in the casket. And what was noticeable in the work was still what is rarest in the work of voluble younger poets, a certain hardness like that of a gem* or cameo, and as it were a sharp keeping of the thing in hand. It was like a portraiture outlined in severe relief, though in itself a wonderful fancy work in a manner, somehow not altogether unlike that of the metal honeysuckle.

For that power of the metal-worker was still guiding his hand, its effect seen at first in a mere word or phrase, as it might be one day in ode or epic and always as with the seal of a master's triumph over matter, agate or steel, which having resisted somewhat on the way and then finally shaped, his thought might well retain its impress forever.

And his capacity, in nowise dwindling hitherto, though in so meagre a soil, suddenly found its opportunity—a fortunate circumstance, while it deferred the more material cares of life, enabled him still in earliest manhood to depart southwards, and visit, at his own humour, those foreign lands, so much longed after, in the company of his chosen friend. It was like coming after years of enforced severity in youth into a great inheritance. That intellectual life within life which had involved for him, so far, a certain bitter self-reliance and a somewhat sad sort of walking by faith, enlarged now rapidly to something ripe and full, like the sudden enrichment of the youthful body itself in its propitious year. It is in this, so poetical a situation, as he tarries awhile for the coming of his friend at a place where he sees the sea for the first time, that the reader is to contemplate him.

He is on the coast of France, not far from the old Norman farm, which however he does not visit as it

35

has passed into the hands of strangers, his father also having died in one of those years which already seem distant, leaving him a small inheritance. The coming even *so* far southwards from the narrow Cumberland valley he felt like a removal in the abstract from North to South. The sparkling light and lovely colours here in the brilliant air blent themselves to a unity very soothing to one's animal spirits. The merely physical exhilaration which came with those smooth winds from the sea, the over-wrought sensibility with which he seemed to appreciate the material elements as it were of their balm and salt, coaxing him into a sort of renewed life, might, perhaps, to an experienced eye, have been the sign of the action already within him of that strange malady which holds so closely of the too-clinging humours of our English climate, which is also, in part, a matter of inheritance, and was established in him by that long tension of spirit to which the distinction of his intellectual quality was due.* But so it was that above all intellectual or poetic enjoyment of the novelties around him there preponderated a wholly physical satisfaction in the quickening impulse of the air, the breath of the sea and sand, weeds in blossom or turning to decay. And as he waited for his friend that they might start on their wanderings together, not unwilling to linger a little among the voices of the toy-like French children at play, all Europe in its priceless art and choicer scenery crowded together, seemed to hang just beyond the horizon in his fancy, like some precious stone, with soft shiftings and variations.

That place with its vast grey, yellow-lichened Norman church, lay amidst the sand dunes grown richly about with wild marigold and yellow horned poppies at the mouth of a river which came down from the tranquil French corn-fields, with a sudden breadth and openness towards the sea in the last few miles of its course. And the boy savoured profoundly all the poetry, the quickening influence for the fancy, of the tidal character of this river, the strong pulse of the invisible sea rising so subtly along its windings, till the blue water far inland almost touched the corn; of the gradual change to a sort of greatness in its character as it came nearer to the coast, dropping one by one all its inland marks till the sheep on the marshy flats and open spaces beside it, must feed on the bitter wild lavender and you might mark the last pale dwarf-rose tree beside the disused boat a-shore.

Then the weird, weather-bleached signals to guide the sailors among the quicksands at the river's mouth became visible; and still through all flowed down the bold current of sweet spring-water distinguishable still by its colour till it rolled under the line of white foam, between the white lighthouses, of the harbour. The long black and white jetties, printed clearly on the warm background of sky and sand between which the river flows out through the sea-gates [   ] give one a dry walk far along the sands stretching away on three sides of one, of a warm yellow colour, variegated by numberless small pools and rillets of blue water, between which the white sea-gulls are running quickly backwards and forwards.

The traces of dark masts seemed almost at rest in the quiet space of sea beyond, you could count the little steepled towns above the white breakers on successive headlands. A group of fishermen in coats of the same soft yellow as the sand start up from the bed of sea-grass where they have been lying at watch, and draw their boat down towards the water along a deeper channel just filled by the returning tide. Perhaps no phase of coast scenery brings the sentiment of the strange life of the sea more intimately home to one than those parts of the coast where at low water the tide falls far away, leaving many miles of sand, dropping out of sight almost, till the hour when laden with new salts and new odours it floods the foundations of the town. How hard when all is at the flood to think of the far-off whisper across the sand! [.] The variety and expansiveness of the peculiar scene witnessed thus for the first time in mature manhood seemed to unseal his sense of the actual life of men as passionate or graceful. Fancies, divinations of a real experience as a thing that might be refulgent with ideal light and satisfy a poetic soul, germinating rapidly in him a warmth, a *souffle*, almost like love towards the friend who was coming, came to him, as the strong air from the waves and the scent of the beanfield met about him

Emerald Uthwart
June-July 1892

We smile at epitaphs—at those recent enough to be read easily: smile, for the most part, at what for the most part is an unreal and often vulgar branch of literature; yet a wide one, with its flowers here or there, such as make us regret now and again not to have gathered more carefully in our wanderings a fair average of the like. Their very simplicity, of course, may set one's thoughts in motion to fill up the scanty tale, and those of the young at least are almost always worth while. At Siena, for instance, in the great Dominican church, even with the impassioned work of Sodoma at hand, you may linger in a certain dimly lit chapel to spell out the black-letter memorials of the German students who died here—*ætatis flore!*—at the University, famous early in the last century:* young nobles chiefly, far from the Rhine from Nuremberg, or Leipsic. Note one in particular! Loving parents, and elder brother meant to record carefully the very days of the lad's poor life—*annos, menses, dies:** sent the order, doubtless, from the distant old castle in the Fatherland, but not quite explicitly: the spaces for the numbers remain still unfilled; and they never came to see. After two centuries the omission is not to be rectified; and the young man's memorial has perhaps its propriety as it stands, with those un-numbered, or numberless, days. "Full of affections," observed, once upon a time, a great lover of boys and young men, speaking to a large company of them:—"full of affections, full of powers, full of occupation, how naturally might the younger part of us especially (more naturally than

41

the older) receive the tidings that there are things to be loved and things to be done which shall never pass away. We feel strong, we feel active, we feel full of life; and these feelings do not altogether deceive us, for we shall live for ever. We see a long prospect before us, for which it is worth while to work, even with much labour; for we are as yet young, and the past portion of our lives is but small in comparison of that which probably remains to us. It is most true! The past years of our life are absolutely beyond proportion small in comparison with those which certainly remain to us."*

In a very different neighbourhood, here at home, in a remote Sussex churchyard, you may read that Emerald Uthwart was born on such a day, "at Chase Lodge,* in this parish; and died there," on a day in the year 18—, aged twenty-six: think, thereupon, of the years of a very English existence passed without a lost week in that bloomy English place, amid its English lawns and flower-beds, its oldish brick and raftered plaster. You may see it still, not far off, on a clearing of the wooded hill-side sloping gradually to the sea. But you think wrong. Emerald Uthwart, in almost unbroken absence from his home, longed greatly for it, but left it early and came back there only to die, in disgrace, as he conceived; of which it was he died there, finding the sense of the place all around him at last, like blessed oil in one's wounds.

How they shook their musk from them!—those gardens, among which the youngest son, but not the youngest child, grew up, little considered till he returned there in those last years. The rippling note of the birds he distinguished so acutely seemed a part of this tree-less place, open freely to sun and air, such as rose and carnation loved, in the midst of the old disafforested chase. Brothers and sisters, all alike were gardeners, methodically intimate with their flowers. You need words compact rather of perfume than of colour to describe them, in nice annual order: terms for perfume, as immediate and definite as red, purple, and yellow. Flowers there were which seemed to yield their sweetest in the faint sea-salt, when the loosening wind was strong from the south-west: some which found their way slowly towards the neighbourhood of the old oaks and beech-trees. Others consorted most freely with the wall-fruit, or seemed made for *pot-pourri* to sweeten the old black mahogany furniture. The sweet-pea stacks loved the broad path through the kitchen garden: the old-fashioned garden azalea was the making of a nose-gay, with its honey which clung to one's finger. There were flowers all the sweeter for a battle with the rain: a flower like aromatic medicine: another like summer lingering into winter; it ripened as fruit does: and another was like August, his own birthday time, dropped into March.

The very mould here, rich old black gardener's earth, was flower-seed; and beyond, the fields, one after another, through the white gates breaking the well-grown hedge-rows, were hardly less garden-like: little velvety fields, little with the true sweet English littleness of our little island, our land of vignettes. Here all was little: the very church where they went to pray, to sit, the ancient Uthwarts sleeping all around outside under the windows, deposited there as quietly as fallen trees on their native soil, and almost unrecorded, as there had been almost nothing to record; where, however, Sunday after Sunday, Emerald Uthwart reads, wondering, the solitary memorial of one soldierly member of his race, who had,—well! who had *not* died here at home, in his bed. How wretched! how fine! how inconceivably great and difficult!—not for him! And yet, amid all its littleness, how large his sense of liberty in the place he, the cadet doomed to leave it—his birth-place, where he is also so early to die—had loved better than any one of them. Enjoying hitherto all the freedom of the

43

almost grown-up brothers, the unrepressed noise, the unchecked hours, the old rooms, all their own way, he is literally without the consciousness of rule. Only, when the long irresponsible day is over, amid the dew, the odours, of summer twilight, they roll their cricket field against to-morrow's game. So it had always been with the Uthwarts: they never went to school. In the great attic he has chosen for himself Emerald awakes,—it was a rule, sanitary, almost medical, never to rouse the children: rises to play betimes; or, if he choose, with window flung open to the roses, the sea, turns to sleep again, deliberately, deliciously, under the fine old blankets.

A rather sensuous boy! you may suppose, amid the wholesome, natural self-indulgence of a very English home. His days began there: it closed again, after an interval of the larger number of them, indulgently, mercifully, round his end. For a while he became its centre, old habits changing, the old furniture re-arranged about him, for the first time in many generations, though he left it now with something like resentment in his heart, as if thrust harshly away, sent *ablactatus a matre*:* made an effort thereon to snap the last thread which bound him to it. Yet it would come back upon him sometimes, amid so different a scene, as through a suddenly opened door, or a rent in the wall, with softer thoughts of his people,—there, or *not* there,—and a sudden, dutiful effort on his part to rekindle wasting affection.

The youngest of four sons, but not the youngest of the family!—you conceive the sort of negligence that creeps over even the kindest maternities, in such case; unless, perhaps, sickness, or the sort of misfortune, making the last first for the affectionate, that brought Emerald back at length to die contentedly, interferes with the way of nature. Little by little he comes to understand that, while the brothers are indulged with lessons at home, are some of them free even of these and placed already in the world, where, however, there remains no place

44

for him, he is to go to school, chiefly for the convenience of others—they are going to be much away from home!—that now for the first time, as he says to himself, an old-English Uthwart is to pass under the yoke. The tutor in the house, meantime, aware of some fascination in the lad, teaches him, at his own irregularly chosen hours, more carefully than the others: exerts all his gifts for the purpose, winning him on almost insensibly to youthful proficiency in those difficult rudiments. See him as he stands, seemingly rooted in the spot where he has come to flower! He departs, however, a few days before the departure of the rest,—some to foreign parts, the brothers, who shut up the old place, to town. For a moment, he makes an effort to figure to himself those coming absences as but exceptional intervals in his life here: he will count the days, going more quickly so: find his pleasure in watching the sands fall, as even the sands of time at school must. In fact, he was scarcely ever to lie at ease here again, till he came to take his final leave of it, lying at his length so. In brief holidays he rejoins his people, anywhere, anyhow, in a sort of hurry and makeshift:—*Flos Parietis!** thus carelessly plucked forth. Emerald Uthwart was born on such a day "at Chase Lodge, in this parish, and died there."

See him then as he stands! counting now the hours that remain, on the eve of that first emigration, and look away next at the other place, which through centuries has been forming to receive him: from those garden-beds, now at their richest, but where all is so winsomely little, to that place of "great matters,"* great stones, great memories out of reach. Why! the Uthwarts had scarcely had more memories than their woods, noiselessly deciduous; or their pre-historic, entirely unprogressive, unrecording forefathers, in, or before, the days of the Druids. Centuries of almost "still" life—of birth, death, and the rest, as merely natural processes—had made them and their home what we find them. Centuries of

45

conscious endeavour, on the other hand, had builded, shaped, and coloured the place, a small cell, which Emerald Uthwart was now to occupy; a place such as our most characteristic English education has rightly tended to "find itself a house" in,—a place full, for those who came within its influence, of a will of its own. Here, everything, one's very games, have gone by rule onwards from the dim old monastic days, and the Benedictine school for novices with the wholesome severities which have descended to our own time. Like its customs,—there's a book in the cathedral archives with the names, for centuries past, of the "scholars" who have missed church at the proper times for going there—like its customs, well-worn yet well-preserved, time-stained, time-engrained, time-mellowed, the venerable Norman or English stones of this austere, beautifully proportioned place look like marble, to which Emerald's softly nurtured being, his careless wild-growth, must now adapt itself, though somewhat painfully recoiling from contact with what seems so hard also, and bright, and cold. From his native world of soft garden touches, carnation and rose (they had been everywhere in those last weeks) where everyone did just what he liked, he was passed now to this world of grey stone; and here it was always the decisive word of command. That old warrior Uthwart's record in the church at home, so fine, yet so wretched, so unspeakably great and difficult! seemed written here everywhere around him, as he stood feeling himself fit only to be taught, to be drilled into, his small compartment; in every movement of his companions, with their quaint confining little cloth gowns: in the keen, clear, well-authorised dominancy of some, the instant submission of others. In fact, by one of our wise English compromises, we still teach our so modern boys the Classics: a lesson in attention and patience, at the least. Nay! by a double compromise, with delightful physiognomic results sometimes, we teach them their pagan Latin and Greek under the shadow of mediæval church-towers, amid the haunts, the traditions, and with something of the discipline, of monasticism; for which, as is noticeable, the English have never wholly lost an early inclination. The French, and others, have swept their scholastic houses empty of it, with pedantic fidelity to their theories. English pedants may succeed in doing the like. But the result of our older method has had its value so far, at least, say! for the careful æsthetic observer. It is of such diagonal influences, through complication of influence, that expression comes, in life, in our culture, in the very faces of men and boys,—of these boys. Nothing could better harmonise present with past than the sight of them just here, as they shout at their games, or recite their lessons, over-arched by the work of mediæval priors, or pass to church meekly, into the seats occupied by the young monks before them.

If summer comes reluctantly to our English shores, it is also apt to linger with us;—its *flora* of red and gold leaves on the branches wellnigh to Christmas: the hot days that surprise you, and persist, though heralded by white mornings, hinting that it is but the year's indulgence so to deal with us. To the fanciful, such days may seem most at home in the places where England has thus preferred to locate the somewhat pensive education of its more favoured youth. As Uthwart passes through the old ecclesiastical city, upon which any more modern touch, modern door or window, seems a thing out of place through negligence, the diluted sunlight itself seems driven along with a sparing trace of gilded vane or red tile in it, under the wholesome active wind from the East coast. The long, finely weathered, leaden roof, and the great square tower, gravely magnificent, emphatic from the first view of it over the grey down above the hop-gardens, the gently-watered meadows, dwarf now everything beside: have the bigness of nature's work, seated up there so steadily amid the winds, as rain and fog and heat pass by. More and more persistently, as he proceeds, in the "Green Court"* at last, they occupy the outlook. He is shown the narrow cubicle in which he is to sleep; and there it still is, with nothing else, in the window-pane, as he lies:—"our tower," the "Angel Steeple,"* noblest of its kind. Here, from morning to night, everything seems challenged to follow the upward lead of its long, bold, "perpendicular" lines. The very place one is in, its stone-work, its empty spaces, invade you; invade all who belong to them, as Uthwart belongs, yielding wholly from the first: seem to question you masterfully as to your purpose in being here at all, amid the great memories of the past, of this school:— challenge you, so to speak, to make moral philosophy one of your acquirements, if you can, and to systematise your vagrant self; which, however, will in any case be here systematised for you. In Uthwart, then, is the plain tablet, for the influences of place to inscribe. Say, if you will, that he is under the power of an "embodied ideal," somewhat repellent, but which he cannot despise. He sits in the schoolroom—ancient, transformed chapel of the pilgrims: sits in the sober white and brown place, at the heavy old desks, carved this way and that, crowded as an old churchyard with forgotten names, side by side with sympathetic, or antipathetic, competitors, as it may chance. In a delightful, exactly measured, quarter of an hour's rest, they come about him, seem to wish to be friends at once, good and bad alike, dull and clever: wonder a little at the name, and the owner. A family name—he explains, good-humouredly: tries to tell some story no one could ever remember precisely of the ancestor from whom it came, the one story of the Uthwarts: is spared; nay! petulantly forbidden to proceed. But the name sticks the faster. Nicknames mark, for the most part, popularity. *Emerald!* so every one called Uthwart, but shortened to *Aldy.* They disperse: flock out into the court: acquaint him hastily with the curiosities of the Precincts, the "dark entry,"* the rich heraldries of the blackened and mouldering cloister, the ruined overgrown spaces where the old monastery stood, the stones of which furnished material for the rambling prebends' houses, now "antediluvian" in their turn: are ready also to climb the scaffold-poles always to be found somewhere about the great church, or dive along the odd, secret passages of the old builders, with quite learned explanations (being proud of, and therefore painstaking, about the place) of architectural periods, of Gothic "late" and "early," layer upon layer, down to round-arched "Norman," like the famous staircase of their school.*

The reader comprehends that Uthwart was come where the *genius loci* was a strong one, with a claim to mould all who enter it to a perfect, uninquiring, willing or unwilling, conformity to itself. On Saturday half-holidays the scholars are taken to church in their surplices, across the court, under the lime-trees: emerge at last up the dark winding passages into the melodious, mellow-lighted space, always three days behind the temperature outside, so thick are the walls;—how warm and nice! how cool and nice! The choir, to which they glide in order to their places below the clergy, seems conspicuously cold and sad. But the empty chapels lying beyond it all about into the distance are a trap on sunny mornings for the clouds of yellow effulgence. The Angel Steeple is a lantern within, and sheds down a flood of the like just beyond the gates. You can peep up into it where you sit, if you dare to gaze about you. If at home there had been nothing great, here, to boyish sense, one seems diminished to nothing at all, amid the grand waves, wave upon wave, of patiently-wrought stone; the daring height, the daring severity, of the innumerable, long, upward, ruled lines, rigidly bent just at last, in due place, into the reserved grace of the perfect Gothic arch; the peculiar daylight which seemed to come from further than the light outside. Next morning they are here again. In contrast to those irregularly broken hours at home, the passive length of things impresses Uthwart now. It develops patience,—that tale of hours, the long chanted English service: our English manner of education is a development of patience, of decorous and mannerly patience. "It is good for a man that he bear the yoke in his youth: he putteth his mouth in the dust, he keepeth silence, because he hath borne it upon him."*—They have this for an anthem; sung, however, to wonderfully cheerful and sprightly music, as if one liked the thought.

The aim of a veritable community, says Plato, is not that this or that member of it should be disproportionately at ease, but that the whole should flourish; though, indeed, such general welfare might come round again to the loyal unit therein, and rest with him, as a privilege of his individual being after all.* The social type he preferred, as we know, was conservative Sparta and its youth; whose unsparing discipline had, doubtless, something to do with the fact that it was the handsomest and best-formed in all Greece. A school is not made for one. It would misrepresent Uthwart's wholly unconscious humility to say that he felt the beauty of the *ascêsis** (we need that Greek word) to which he not merely finds himself subject, but as under a fascination submissively yields himself, although another might have been aware of the charm of it, half ethic, half physical, as visibly effective in him. Its peculiarity would have lain in the expression of a stress upon him and his customary daily existence, beyond what any definitely proposed issue of it, at least for the moment, explained. Something of that is involved in the very idea of a classical education, at least for such as he; in its seeming indirectness or lack of purpose, amid so much difficulty, as contrasted with forms of education more obviously useful or practical. He found himself in a system of fixed rules, amid which, it might be, some of his own tendencies and inclinations would die out of him through disuse. The confident word of command, the instantaneous obedience expected, the enforced silence, the very games that go by rule, a sort of hardness natural to wholesome English youths when they come together, but here *de rigueur* as a point of good manners:—he accepts all these without hesitation; the early hours also, naturally distasteful to him, which gave to actual morning, to all that had passed in it, when in more self-conscious mood he looked back on the morning of life, a preponderance, a disproportionate place there, adding greatly to the effect of its dreamy distance from him at this later time:—an *ideal* quality, he might have said, had he ever used such words as that.

Uthwart duly passes his examination; and, in their own chapel in the transept of the choir, lighted up late for evening prayer after the long day of trial, is received to the full privileges of a Scholar with the accustomed Latin words:—*Introitum tuum, et exitum tuum, custodiat Dominus!** He takes them, not to heart, but rather to mind, as few, if they so much as heard them, were wont to do: ponders them for a while. They seem scarcely meant for him,—words like those! increase, however, his sense of responsibility to the place, of which he is now more exclusively than before a part—that he belongs to it, its great memories, great dim purposes: deepen the consciousness he had on first coming hither of a demand in the world about him, whereof the very stones are emphatic, to which no average human creature could be sufficient; of reproof, reproaches, of this or that in himself.

It was repeated, there was a funny belief, at school that Aldy Uthwart had no feeling and was incapable of tears. They never came to him, certainly when, at nights for the most part, the very touch of home, so soft, yet so indifferent to him, reached him, with a sudden

51

opulent rush of garden perfumes: came at the rattling of the window-pane in the wind, with anything that expressed distance from the bare white walls around him here. He thrust it from him brusquely, being of a practical turn, and, though somewhat sensuous, wholly without sentimentality. There is something, however, in the lad's soldier-like, impassible self-command, in his sustained expression of a certain indifference to things, which awakes suddenly all the sentiment, the poetry, latent hitherto in another,—James Stokes, the prefect, his immediate superior: awakes for the first time into ample flower something of genius in a seemingly plodding scholar, and therewith also something of the waywardness popularly thought to belong to genius. *Preceptores, condiscipuli,** alike, marvel at a sort of delicacy coming into the habits, the person, of that tall, bashful, broad-shouldered, very Kentish, lad; so unaffectedly nevertheless, that it is understood after all to be but the smartness properly significant of change to early manhood, like the down on his lip. Wistful anticipations of manhood are in fact aroused in him, thoughts of the future: his ambition takes effective outline. The well-worn, perhaps conventional, beauties of their "dead" Greek and Latin books, associated directly now with the living companion beside him, really shine for him at last with their pristine freshness: seem more than to fulfil their claim upon the patience, the attention, of modern youth. He notices as never before minute points of meaning in Homer, in Virgil: points out thus, for instance, to his junior, one day in the sunshine, how the Greeks had a special word for the Fate which accompanied one who would come to a violent end. The common Destinies of men, $Mo\bar{\iota}\rho\alpha\iota$, *Mœræ*—they accompanied all men indifferently. But $K\acute{\eta}\rho$ the extraordinary Destiny, one's Doom, had a scent for distant blood-shedding; and, to be in at a sanguinary death, one of their number came forth to the very cradle, followed persistently all the way, over the waves, through powder and shot, through the rose-gardens;—where not? Looking back, one might trace the red footsteps all along, side by side. (Emerald Uthwart, you remember, was to "die there," of lingering sickness, in disgrace, as he fancied, while the word glory came to be softly whispered of them and of their end.) Classic felicities, the choice expressions, with which James Stokes has so patiently stored his memory, furnish now a dainty embroidery upon every act, every change in time or place, of their daily life in common. He finds the Greek or the Latin model of their antique friendship or tries to find it, in the books they read together. None fits exactly. It is of military glory they are really thinking, amid those ecclesiastical surroundings, where, however, surplices and uniforms are often mingled together: how they will lie, in costly glory, costly to them, side by side, (as they work and walk and play now, side by side,) in the cathedral aisle, with a tattered flag perhaps above them, and under a single epitaph, like that of those two older scholars, Ensigns, *Signiferi*, in their respective regiments, *in hac ecclesiâ pueri instituti*,* with the sapphic stanza in imitation of the Horace they had learned here, written by their old master.

Horace!—he was, had been always, the idol of their school: to know him by heart, to translate him into effective English idiom, have an apt phrase of his instinctively on one's lips for every occasion. That boys should be made to spout him under penalties, would have seemed doubtless to that sensitive, vain, winsome poet, even more than to grim Juvenal, quite the sorriest of fates: might have seemed not so bad, however, could he, from the "ashes" so persistently in his thoughts, have peeped on these English boys, row upon row, with black or golden heads, repeating him in the fresh morning, and observed how well for once the thing was done: how well he was understood by English James Stokes, feeling the old "fire" really "quick" still, under the influence which now in truth quickened, enlivened, everything around him. The old heathen's way of looking at things, his melodious expression of it, blends, or contrasts, itself oddly with the everyday detail, with the very stones, the Gothic stones, of a world he could hardly have conceived, its mediæval surroundings, their half-clerical life here. Yet not so inconsistently after all! The builders of these aisles and cloisters had known and valued as much of him as they could come by in their own un-instructed time; had built up their intellectual edifice more than they were aware of from fragments of pagan thought, as, quite consciously, they constructed their churches of old Roman bricks and pillars, or frank imitations of them. One's day, then, began with him, for all alike, Sundays of course excepted,—with an Ode, learned over-night by the prudent, who, observing how readily the words which send us to sleep cling to the brain and seem an inherent part of it next morning, kept him under their pillows. Prefects, without a book, heard the repetition of the Juniors, must be able to correct their blunders. Odes and Epodes, thus acquired, were a score of days and weeks; alcaic and sapphic verses like a bead-roll for counting off the time that intervened before the holidays. Time—that tardy servant of youthful appetite—brought them soon enough to the point where they desired in vain "to see one of" those days, erased now so willingly; and sentimental James Stokes has already a sense that this "pause 'twixt cup and lip"* of life is really worth pausing over, worth deliberation:—all this poetry, yes! poetry, surely, of their alternate work and play; light and shade, call it! Had it been, after all, a life in itself less commonplace than theirs,—that life, the trivial details of which their Horace had touched so daintily, gilded with real gold words?

Regular, submissive, dutiful to play also, Aldy meantime enjoys his triumphs in the Green Court; loves best, however, to run a paper-chase* afar over the marshes, till you come in sight, or within scent, of the sea, in the autumn twilight; and his dutifulness to games at least had its full reward. A wonderful hit of his at cricket was long remembered: right over the lime trees on to the cathedral roof, was it? or over the roof, and onward into space, circling there independently, minutely, as *Sidus Cantiorum.** A comic poem on it in Latin, and a pretty one in English, were penned by James Stokes, still not so serious but that he forgets time altogether one day, in a manner the converse of exemplary in a prefect, whereupon Uthwart, his companion as usual, manages to take all the blame, and the due penalty next morning. Stokes accepted the sacrifice the more readily, believing—he too—that Aldy was "incapable of pain." What surprised those who were in the secret was that, when it was over, he rose, and facing the headmaster—could it be insolence? or was it the sense of untruthfulness in his friendly action, or sense of the universal peccancy of all boys and men?—said submissively, "And now, sir, that I have taken my punishment, I hope you will forgive my fault."

Submissiveness!—It had the force of genius with Emerald Uthwart. In that very matter he had but yielded to a senior against his own inclination. What he felt in Horace was the sense, original, active, personal, of "things too high for *me!*" the sense, not really unpleasing to him, of an unattainable height here too, in this royal felicity of utterance, this literary art, the minute cares of which had been really designed for the minute carefulness of a disciple such as this,—all attention. Well! the sense of authority, of a large intellectual authority over us, impressed anew day after day, of some impenetrable glory round "the masters of those who know,"* is, of course, one of the effects we look for from a classical education:—that, and a full estimate of the preponderating value of the manner of the doing of it in the thing done; which again, for ingenuous youth, is an encouragement of good manners on its part,—"I behave myself orderly." Just at those points, scholarship attains something of a religious colour. And in that place, religion, religious system, its claim to overpower one, presented itself in a way of which even the least serious by nature could not be unaware. Their great church, its customs and traditions, formed an element in that *esprit de corps* into which the boyish mind throws itself so readily. Afterwards, in very different scenes, the sentiment of that place would come back upon him, as if resentfully, by contrast with the conscious or unconscious profanities of others, crushed out about him straightway, by the shadow of awe, the minatory flash, felt around his unopened lips, in the glance, the changed manner. Not to be "occupied with great matters" recommends in heavenly places, as we know, the souls of some. Yet there were a few to whom it seemed unfortunate that religion whose flag Uthwart would have borne in hands so pure, touched him from first to last, and till his eyes were finally closed on this world, only, again, as a thing immeasurable, surely not meant for the like of him: its high claims, to which no one could be equal: its reproaches. He would scarcely have proposed to "enter into" such matters: was constitutionally shy of them. His submissiveness, you see, *was* a kind of genius: made him, therefore, of course, unlike those around him: was a secret: a thing, you might say, "which no one knoweth, saving he that receiveth it."*

Thus repressible, self-restrained, always concurring with the influence, the claim upon him, the rebuke, of others, in the bustle of school life he did not count even with those who knew him best, with those who taught him, for the intellectual capacity he really had. In every generation of schoolboys there are a few who find out, almost for themselves, the beauty and power of good literature, even in the literature they must read

56

perforce; and this, in turn, is but the handsel of a beauty and power still active in the actual world, should they have the good fortune, or, rather, acquire the skill, to deal with it properly. It has something of the stir and unction—this intellectual awaking with a leap—of the coming of love. So it was with Uthwart about his seventeenth year. He felt it, felt the intellectual passion, like the pressure outward of wings within him,—ἡ πτεροῦ δύναμις, says Plato, in the *Phædrus*:* but again, as some do with everyday love, withheld, restrained himself: the status of a freeman in the world of intellect can hardly be for him. The sense of intellectual ambition, ambitious thoughts such as sweeten the toil of some of those about him, coming to him once in a way, he is frankly recommended to put them aside, and acquiesces: puts them from him once for all, as he could do with besetting thoughts and feelings, his preferences (as he had put aside soft thoughts of home as a disobedience to rule) and with a countenance more good-humoured than ever, an absolute placidity. It is fit he should be treated sparingly in this matter of intellectual enjoyment. He is made to understand that there is at least a score of others as good scholars as he. He will have of course all the pains, but must not expect the prizes, of his work; of his loyal, incessant, cheerful industry.

But only see him as he goes. It is as if he left music, delightfully throbbing music, or flowers, behind him, as he passes, careless of them, unconsciously, through the world, the school, the precincts, the old city. Strangers' eyes, resting on him by chance, are deterred for a while, even among the rich sights of the venerable place, as he walks out and in, in his prim gown and purple-tasselled cap; goes in, with the stream of sunlight, through the black shadows of the mouldering Gothic gateway, like youth's very self, eternal, immemorial, eternally renewed, about those immemorially ancient stones. "Young Apollo!" people say—people who have pigeon

57

holes for their impressions, watching the slim, trim figure with the exercise books. His very dress seems touched with Hellenic fitness to the healthy youthful form. "Golden-haired, scholar Apollo!" they repeat, foolishly, ignorantly. He was better: was more like a real portrait of a real young Greek, like *Tryphon, Son of Eutychos*,* for instance, (as friends remembered him with regret, as you may see him still on his tombstone in the British Museum,) alive among the paler physical and intellectual lights of modern England, under the old monastic stonework of the Middle Age. That theatrical old Greek god never took the expressiveness, the lines of delicate meaning, such as were come into the face of the English lad, the physiognomy of his race; ennobled now, as if by the writing, the signature, there, of a grave intelligence, by grave information and a subdued will, though without a touch of melancholy in this "best of playfellows." A musical composer's notes, we know, are not themselves till the fit executant comes, who can put all they may be into them. The somewhat unmeaningly handsome facial type of the Uthwarts, moulded to a mere animal or physical perfection through wholesome centuries, is breathed on now, informed, by the touches, traces, complex influences from past and present a thousandfold, crossing each other in this late century, and yet at unity in the simple law of the system to which he is now subject. Coming thus upon an otherwise vigorous and healthy nature, an untainted physique, and limited by it, those combining mental influences leave the firm unconscious simplicity of the boyish nature still unperplexed. The sisters, their friends, when he comes rarely upon them in foreign places, are proud of the schoolboy's company,—to walk at his side; the brothers, when he sees them for a day, more considerate than of old. Everywhere he leaves behind him an odd regret for his presence, as he in turn wonders sometimes at the deference paid to one so unimportant as himself by those he meets by accident perhaps; at the ease, for example, with which he attains to the social privileges denied to others.

They tell him, he knows it already, he would "do for the army." "Yes! that would suit you," people observe at once, when he tells them what "he is to be": undoubtedly suit him, that dainty, military, very English kind of pride, in seeming precisely what one is, neither more nor less. And the first mention of Uthwart's purpose defines also the vague outlooks of James Stokes, who will be a soldier too. Uniforms, their scarlet and white and blue, spruce leather and steel, and gold lace, enlivening the old oak stalls at service time,—uniforms and surplices were always close together here, where a military garrison had been established in the suburbs for centuries past, and there were always sons of its officers in the school. If you stole out of an evening, it was like a stage scene; nay! like the Middle Age itself, with this multitude of soldiers mingling in the crowd which filled the unchanged, gabled streets. A military tradition had been continuous, from the days of crusading knights who lay humbly on their backs in the "Warriors' Chapel"* to the time of the civil wars, when a certain heroic youth of eighteen was brought to rest there, onward to Dutch and American wars, and to Harry, and Geoffrey, and another James also, *in hac ecclesiâ pueri instituti*. It was not so long since one of them sat on those very benches in the sixth form: had come back and entered the school, in full uniform, to say good-bye! Then the "colours" of his regiment had been brought, to be deposited by Dean and Canons in the cathedral; and a few weeks later they had passed, scholars and the rest, in long procession, to deposit Ensign —— himself there under his flag, or what remained of it, a sorry, tattered fringe, along the staff he had borne out of the battle at the cost of his life, as a little tablet explained. There were others in similar terms. Alas! for that extraordinary, peculiarly-named,

59

Destiny, or Doom, appointed to walk side by side with one or another, aware from the first, but never warning him, till the random or well-considered shot comes.*

Meantime however, the University, with work in preparation thereto, fills up the thoughts, the hours, of these would-be soldiers, of James Stokes, and therefore of Emerald Uthwart, through the long summer-time, till the Green Court is fragrant with lime-blossom and speech-day comes, on which, after their flower-service and sermon from an old comrade, Emerald surprises masters and companions by the fine quality of a recitation; still more when "Scholar Stokes" and he are found bracketed together as "Victors"* of the school, who will proceed together to Oxford. His speech in the Chapter-house was from that place in Homer, where the soul of the lad Elpenor, killed by accident, entreats Ulysses for due burial rites. "Fix my oar over my grave," he says, "the oar I rowed with when I lived, when I went with my companions."* And in effect what surprised, charmed the hearers was the scruple with which those naturally graceful lips dealt with every word, every syllable, put upon them. He seemed to be thinking only of his author, except for just so much of self-consciousness as was involved in the fact that he seemed also to be speaking a little against his will, like a monk, it might be said, who sings in choir with a really fine voice, but at the bidding of his superior, and counting the notes all the while till his task be done, because his whole nature revolts from so much as the bare opportunity for personal display. It was his duty to speak on the occasion. They had always been great in speech-making, in theatricals, from before the days when the Puritans destroyed the Dean's "Great Hall" because "the King's Scholars had profaned it by acting plays there"; and that peculiar note or accent, as being conspicuously free from the egotism which vulgarises most of us, seemed to befit the person of Emerald, impressing weary listeners pleasantly as a novelty in that kind. Singular!—The words, because seemingly forced from him, had been worth hearing. The cheers, the "Kentish Fire," of their companions might have broken down the crumbling black arches of the old cloister, or roused the dead under foot, as the "Victors" came out of the Chapter-house side by side: side by side also out of that delightful period of their life at school, to proceed in due course to the University.

They left it precipitately, after brief residence there, taking advantage of a sudden outbreak of war to join the army at once, regretted—James Stokes for his high academic promise, Uthwart for a quality, or group of qualities, not strictly to be defined. He seemed, in short, to harmonise by their combination in himself all the various qualities proper to a large and varied community of youths of nineteen or twenty, to which, when actually present there, he was felt from hour to hour to be indispensable. In fact school habits and standards had survived in a world not so different from that of school for those who are faithful to its type. When he looked back upon it a little later, college seemed to him, seemed indeed at the time, had he ventured to admit it, a strange prolongation of boyhood, in its provisional character, the narrow limitation of its duties and responsibility, the very divisions of one's day, the routine of play and work, its formal, perhaps pedantic rules. The veritable plunge from youth into manhood came when one passed finally through those old Gothic gates, from a somewhat dreamy or problematic preparation for it, into the world of peremptory facts. A college, like a school, is not made for one; and as Uthwart sat there, still but a scholar, still reading with care the books prescribed for him by others—Greek and Latin books— the contrast between his own position and that of the majority of his coevals already at the business of life impressed itself sometimes with an odd sense of unreality in the place around him. Yet the schoolboy's sensitive awe for the great things of the intellectual world had but matured itself, and was at its height here amid this larger competition, which left him more than ever to find in doing his best submissively the sole reward of so doing. He needs now in fact less repression than encouragement not to be a "passman,"* as he may if he likes, acquiescing in a lowly measure of culture which certainly will not manufacture Miltons, nor turn serge into silk, broom-blossom into verbenas, but only, perhaps not so faultily, leave Emerald Uthwart and the like of him essentially what they are. "He holds his book in a peculiar way," notes in manuscript one of his tutors: "holds on to it with both hands: clings as if from below, just as his tough little mind clings to the sense of the Greek words he can English so closely, precisely." Again, as at school, he had put his neck under the yoke; though he has now also much reading quite at his own choice; by preference, when he can come by such, about the place where he finds himself, about the earlier youthful occupants, if it might be, of his own quaint rooms on the second floor just below the roof; of what he can see from his windows in the old black front eastwards, with its inestimable *patina* of ancient smoke and weather and natural decay (when you look close the very stone is a composite of minute dead bodies) relieving heads like his so effectively on summer mornings. On summer nights the scent of the hay, the wild-flowers, comes across the narrow fringe of town to right and left: seems to come from beyond the Oxford meadows, with sensitive, half-repellent thoughts from the gardens at home. He looks down upon the green square with the slim quaint black young figures that cross it on the way to chapel on yellow Sunday mornings, or upwards to the dome, the spire: can watch them closely in freakish moonlight, or flickering softly by an occasional bonfire in the quadrangle behind him. Yet how hard, how forbidding sometimes, under a late stormy sky, the scheme of black, white, and grey, to which the group of ancient buildings could attune itself. And what he reads most readily is of the military life that intruded itself so oddly, during the Civil War,* into these half-monastic places, till the timid old academic world scarcely knew itself. He treasures, then, every incident which connects a soldier's coat with any still recognisable object, wall, or tree, or garden-walk; that walk, for instance, under Merton garden where young Colonel Windebank was shot for a traitor.* His body lies in Saint Mary Magdalen's churchyard. Unassociated to such incident, the mere beauties of the place counted at the moment for less than in retrospect. It was almost retrospect even now, with an anticipation of regret, in rare moments of solitude perhaps, when the oars splashed far up the narrow streamlets through the fields on May evenings among the fritillaries—does the reader know them? that strange remnant just here of a richer extinct flora—dry flowers, though with a drop of dubious honey in each. Snakes' heads, the rude call them, for their shape, scale-marked too, and in colour like rusted blood, as if they grew from some forgotten battle-field, the bodies, the rotten armour,—yet delicate, beautiful, waving proudly. In truth the memory of Oxford made almost everything he saw after it seem vulgar. But he feels also nevertheless, characteristically, that such local pride (*fastus** he terms it) is proper only for those whose occupations are wholly congruous with it: for the gifted, the freemen who can enter into the genius, who possess the liberty, of the place: that it has a reproach in it for the outsider, which comes home to him.

Here again then as he passes through the world, so delightfully to others, they tell him, as if weighing him, his very self, against his merely scholastic capacity and effects, that he would "do for the army"; which he is now wholly glad to hear, for from first to last, through all his successes there, the army had still been scholar

Stokes's choice, and he had no difficulty, as the reader sees, in keeping Uthwart also faithful to first intentions. Their names were already entered for commissions; but the war breaking out afresh, information reaches them suddenly one morning that they may join their regiment forthwith. Bidding good-bye therefore, gladly, hastily, they set out with as little delay as possible for Flanders;* and passing the old school by their nearest road thither, stay for an hour, find an excuse for coming into the hall in uniform, with which it must be confessed they seem thoroughly satisfied—Uthwart quite perversely at ease in the stiff make of his scarlet jacket with black facings—and so pass onward on their way to Dover, Dunkirk, they scarcely know whither finally, among the featureless villages, the long monotonous lines of the windmills, the poplars, blurred with cold fogs, but marking the roads through the snow which covers the endless plain, till they come in sight at last of the army in motion, like machines moving—how little it looked on that endless plain! pass on their rapid way to fame, to unpurchased promotion, as a matter of course to responsibility also, till, their fortune turning upon them, they miscarry in the latter fatally. They joined, in fact, a distinguished regiment in a gallant army, immediately after a victory in those Flemish regions: shared its encouragement as fully as if they had had a share in its perils; the high character of the young officers consolidating itself easily, pleasantly for them, till the hour of an act of thoughtless bravery, almost the sole irregular or undisciplined act of Uthwart's life, he still following his senior—criminal, however, to the military conscience, under the actual circumstances, and in an enemy's country. The faulty thing was done, certainly, with a scrupulous, a characteristic completeness on their part; and with their prize actually in hand, an old weather-beaten flag such as hung in the cathedral aisle at school, they bethought them for the first time of its price, with misgivings now in rapid growth, as they return to their posts as nearly as may be, for the division has been ordered forward in their brief absence, to find themselves under arrest, with that damning proof of heroism, of guilt, in their possession, relinquished however, along with the swords they will never handle again—toys, idolised toys of our later youth, we weep at the thought of never to be handled again!—as they enter the prison to await summary trial next day on the charge of wantonly deserting their posts while in position of high trust in time of war.

The full details of what had happened could have been told only by one or other of themselves: by Uthwart best, in the somewhat matter-of-fact and prosaic journal he had managed to keep from the first, noting there the incidents of each successive day, as if in anticipation of its possible service by way of *pièce justificative,** should such become necessary, attesting hour by hour their single-hearted devotion to soldierly duty. Had a draughtsman equally truthful, or equally "realistic," as we say, accompanied them and made a like use of his pencil, he might have been mistaken at home for an artist aiming at "effect," by skilful "arrangements" to tickle people's interest in the spectacle of war—the sudden ruin of a village street, the heap of bleeding horses in the half-ploughed field, the gaping bridges, hand or face of the dead peeping from a hastily made grave at the roadside, smoke-stained rents in cottage-walls, ignoble ruin everywhere—ignoble but for its frank expression.

But you find in Uthwart's journal, side by side with those ugly patches, very precise and unadorned records of their common gallantry, the more effective indeed for their simplicity: and not of gallantry only, but of the long-sustained patience also, the essential monotony of military life, even on a campaign. Peril, good-luck, promotion, the grotesque hardships which leave them smart as ever, as if, so others observe, dust and mire

65

wouldn't hold on them, so "spick and span" they were, more especially on days of any exceptional risk or effort, the great confidence reposed in them at last: all is noted, till, with a little quiet pride, he records a gunshot wound which keeps him a month alone in hospital wearily; and, at last, its hasty but seemingly complete healing.

Following, leading, resting sometimes perforce, amid gun-shots, putrefying wounds, green corpses, they never lacked good spirits, any more than the birds warbling perennially afresh, as they will, over such gangrened places, or the grass which so soon covers them. And at length fortune, their misfortune, perversely determined that heroism should take the form of patience under the walls of an unimportant frontier town, with old Vauban fortifications seemingly made only for appearance sake, like the work in the trenches—gardener's work! round about the walls they are called upon to superintend day after day. It was like a calm at sea, delaying one's passage, one's purpose in being on board at all, a dead calm, yet with an awful feeling of tension, intolerable at last for those who were still all athirst for action. How dumb and stupid the place seemed, in its useless defiance of conquerors, anxious, for reasons not apparent indeed, but in holding to which they were undoubtedly within their rights, not to blow it at once into the air—the steeple, the perky weathercock—to James Stokes in particular, always eloquent in action, longing for heroic effort, and ready to pay its price, maddened now by the palpable imposture in front of him morning after morning, as he demonstrates conclusively to Uthwart, seduced at last from the clearer sense of duty and discipline, not by the demonstrated ease, but rather by the apparent difficulty of what Stokes proposes to do. They might have been deterred by recent example. Colonel ——, who, as every one knew, had actually gained a victory by disobeying orders, had not been suffered to remain in the army of which he was an ornament. It was easy in fact for both, though it seemed the heroic thing, to dash through the calm with delightful sense of active powers renewed; to pass into the beleaguered town with a handful of men, and no loss, after a manner the feasibility of which Stokes had explained acutely but in vain at headquarters. He proved it to Uthwart at all events, and a few others. Delightful heroism! delightful self-indulgence! It was delayed for a moment by orders to move forward at last, with hopes checked almost immediately after by a counter-mand, bringing them right round their stupid dumb enemy to the same wearisome position once again, to the trenches and the rest, but with their thirst for action only stimulated the more. How great the disappointment! encouraging a certain laxity of discipline that had prevailed about them of late. They take advantage, however, of a vague phrase in their instructions; determine in haste to proceed on their plan as carefully, as sparingly of the lives of others as may be; detach a small company, hazarding thereby an algebraically certain scheme at headquarters of victory or secure retreat, which embraced the entire country in its calculations; detach themselves; finally pass into the place, and out again with their prize, themselves secure. Themselves only could have told the details—the intensely pleasant, the glorious sense of movement renewed once more; of defiance, just for once, of a seemingly stupid control: their dismay at finding their company led forward by others, their own posts deserted, their handful of men—nowhere!

In an ordinary trial at law, the motives, every detail of so irregular an act might have been weighed, changing the colour of it. Their general character would have told in their favour, but actually told against them now: they had but won an exceptional trust to betray it. Martial courts exist not for consideration, but for vivid exemplary effect and prompt punishment. "There is a kind of tribunal incidental to service in the field," writes another diarist, who may tell in his own words what remains to be told. "This court," he says, "may consist of three staff-officers only, but has the power of sentencing to death. On the —st two young officers of the —th regiment, in whom, it appears, unusual confidence had been placed, were brought before this court on the charge of desertion and wantonly exposing their company to danger. They were found guilty, and that the proper penalty is death, to be inflicted next morning before the regiment marches. The delinquents were understood to have appealed to a general court-martial; desperately, at last, to 'the judgment of their country'; but were held to have no *locus standi** for any appeal whatever under the actual circumstances. As a civilian I cannot but doubt the justice, whatever may be thought of the expediency of such a summary process in regard to the capital penalty. The regiment to which the culprits belonged, with some others, was quartered for the night in the *faubourg* of Saint ——, recently under blockade by a portion of our forces. I was awoke at daybreak by the sound of marching. The morning was a particularly clear one, though, as the sun was not yet risen, it looked grey and sad along the empty street, up which a party of grey soldiers were passing with steady pace. I knew for what purpose.

"The whole of the force in garrison here had already marched to the place of execution, the immense courtyard of a monastery, surrounded irregularly by ancient buildings like those of some cathedral precincts I have seen in England. Here the soldiers then formed three sides of a great square, a grave having been dug on the fourth side. Shortly afterwards the funeral procession came up. First came the band of the —th, playing the Dead March; next the firing party, consisting of twelve non-commissioned officers; then the coffins, followed immediately by the unfortunate prisoners, accompanied by a chaplain. Slowly and sadly did the mournful procession approach, when it passed through three sides of the square, the troops having been previously faced inwards, and then halted opposite to the grave. The proceedings of the court-martial were then read; and the elder prisoner having been blindfolded was ordered to kneel down on his coffin, which had been placed close to the grave, the firing party taking up a position exactly opposite at a few yards' distance. The poor fellow's face was deadly pale, but he had marched his last march as steadily as ever I saw a man step, and bore himself throughout most bravely, though an oddly mixed expression passed over his countenance when he was directed to remove himself from the side of his companion, shaking his hand first. At this moment there was hardly a dry eye, and several young soldiers fainted, numberless as must be the scenes of horror which even they have witnessed during these last months. At length the chaplain, who had remained praying with the prisoner, quietly withdrew, and at a given signal, but without word of command, the muskets were levelled, a volley was fired, and the body of the unfortunate man sprang up, falling again on his back. One shot had purposely been reserved; and as the presiding officer thought he was not quite dead, a musket was placed close to his head and fired. All was now over; but the troops having been formed into columns, were marched close by the body as it lay on the ground, after which it was placed in one of the coffins and buried.

"I had almost forgotten his companion, the younger and more fortunate prisoner, though I could scarcely tell, as I looked at him, whether his fate was really preferable in leaving his own rough coffin unoccupied behind him there. Lieutenant (I think Edward) Uthwart, as being the younger of the two offenders, 'by the mercy of the court' had his sentence commuted to dismissal from the army with disgrace. A colour-sergeant then advanced with the former officer's sword, a remarkably fine one, which he thereupon snapped in sunder over the prisoner's head as he knelt. After this the prisoner's regimental coat was handed forward and put upon him, the epaulettes and buttons being then torn off and flung to a distance. This part of such sentences is almost invariably spared; but, I suppose through unavoidable haste, was on the present occasion somewhat rudely carried out. I shall never forget the expression of this man's countenance, though I have seen many sad things in the course of my profession. He had the sort of good looks which always rivet attention, and in most minds friendly interest; and now, amid all his pain and bewilderment, bore a look of humility and submission as he underwent those extraordinary details of his punishment, which touched me very oddly with a sort of desire (I cannot otherwise express it) to share his lot, to be actually in his place for a moment. Yet, alas!—no! say rather Thank Heaven! the nearest approach to that look I have seen has been on the face of those whom I have known from circumstances to be almost incapable at the time of any feeling whatever. I would have offered him pecuniary aid, supposing he needed it, but it was impossible. I went on with the regiment, leaving the poor wretch to shift for himself: Heaven knows how, the state of the country being what it is. He might join the enemy!"

What money Uthwart had about him had, in fact, passed that morning into the hands of his guards. To tell what followed would be to accompany him on a roundabout and really aimless journey, the details of which he could never afterwards recall. See him lingering for morsels of food at some shattered farmstead, or assisted by others almost as wretched as himself, sometimes without his asking. In his worn military dress he seems a part of the ruin under which he creeps for a night's rest

70

as darkness comes on. He actually came round again to the scene of his disgrace, of the execution: looked in vain for the precise spot where he had knelt: then, almost envying him who lay there, for the unmarked grave: passed over it perhaps unrecognised for some change in that terrible place, or rather in himself: wept then as never before in his life: dragged himself on once more, till suddenly the whole country seems to move under the rumour, the very thunder, of "the crowning victory," as he is made to understand. Falling in with the tide of its heroes returning to English shores, his vagrant footsteps are at last directed homewards. He finds himself one afternoon at the gate, turning out of the quiet Sussex road, through the fields for whose safety he had fought with so much of undeniable gallantry and approval.

On that July afternoon the gardens, the woods, mounted in flawless sweetness all round him as he stood, to meet the circle of a flawless sky. Not a cloud: not a motion on the grass! At the first he had intended to return home no more; and it had been a proof of his great dejection that he sent at last, as best he could, for money. They knew his fate already by report, and were touched naturally when that had followed on the record of his honours. Had it been possible they would have set forth at any risk to meet, to seek him: were waiting now for the weary one to come to the gate, ready with their oil and wine, to speak metaphorically, and from this time forth underwent his charm to the utmost—the charm of an exquisite character, felt in some way to be inseparable from his person, his characteristic movements, touched also now with seemingly irreparable sorrow. For his part, savouring here the last sweets of the sensible world, it was as if he, the lover of roses, had never before been aware of them at all. The original softness of his temperament, against which the sense of greater things thrust upon him had successfully reacted, asserted itself again now as he lay at ease, the ease well merited by his deeds, his sorrows. That he was going to die moved those about him to humour this mood, to soften all things to his touch; and looking back he might have pronounced those four last years of doom the happiest of his life. The memory of the grave into which he had gazed so steadily on the execution morning, into which, as he feels, one half of himself had then descended, does not lessen his shrinking from the fate before him, yet fortifies him to face it manfully, gives a sort of fraternal familiarity to death: in a few weeks' time this battle too is fought out; it is as if the thing were ended. The delightful summer heat, the freshness it enhances—he contrasts such things no longer with the sort of place to which he is hastening. The possible duration of life for him was indeed uncertain, the future to some degree indefinite; but as regarded any fairly distant date, anything like a term of years, from the first there had been no doubt at all: he would be no longer here. Meantime it was like a delightful few days' additional holiday from school, with which, perforce, one must be content at last; or as though he had not been pardoned on that terrible morning, but only reprieved for two or three years. Yet how large a proportion they would have seemed in the whole sum of his years. He would have liked to lie finally in the garden among departed pets, dear dead dogs and horses: faintly proposes it one day; but after a while comprehends the churchyard, with its white spots in the distant flowery view, as filling harmoniously its own proper place there. The weary soul seemed to be settling deeper into the body and the earth it came of, into the condition of the flowers, the grass, proper creatures of the earth to which he is returning. The saintly vicar visits him considerately: is repelled with politeness: goes on his way, pondering inwardly what kind of place there might be, in any possible scheme of another world, for so absolutely unspiritual a subject. In fact, as the breath of the infinite world came about him, he clung all the faster to the beloved finite things still in contact with him: he had successfully hidden from his eyes all beside.

His reprieve, however, lasted long enough, after all, for a certain change of opinion of immense weight to him—a revision or reversal of judgment. It came about in this way. When peace was arranged, with question of rewards, pensions, and the like, certain battles, or incidents therein, were fought over again, sometimes in the highest places of debate. On such an occasion a certain speaker cites the case of Lieutenant James Stokes and another, as being *"pessimi exempli"*:* whereupon a second speaker gets up, prepared with full detail, insists, brings that incidental matter to the front for an hour, tells his unfortunate friend's story so effectively, pathetically, that, as happens with our countrymen, they repent. The matter gets into the newspapers, and, coming thus into sympathetic public view, something like glory wins from Emerald Uthwart his last touch of animation. Just not too late he received the offer of a commission: kept the letter there open within sight. Aldy, who "never shed tears and was incapable of pain," in his great physical weakness, wept—shall we say for the second time in his life? A less excitement would have been more favourable to any chance there might be of the patient's surviving. In fact the old gun-shot wound, wrongly thought to be cured, which had caused the one illness of his life, is now drawing out what remains of it, as he feels with a kind of odd satisfaction and pride— his old glorious wound! And then, as of old, an absolute submissiveness comes over him, as he gazes round at the place, the relics of his uniform, the letter lying there. It was as if there was nothing more that could be said. Accounts thus settled, he stretched himself in the bed he had occupied as a boy, more completely at his ease than since the day when he had left home for the first time. Respited from death once, he was twice believed to be dead before the date actually registered on his tomb. "What will it matter a hundred years hence?" they used to ask by way of sorry comfort in boyish troubles at school, overwhelming at the moment. Was that in truth part of a certain revelation of the inmost truth of things to "babes," such as we have heard of? What did it matter—the gifts, the good-fortune, its terrible withdrawal, the long agony? Emerald Uthwart would have been all but a centenarian to-day.

Postscript, from the Diary of a Surgeon, August —th, 18—.

I was summoned by letter into the country to perform an operation on the dead body of a young man, formerly an officer in the army. The cause of death is held to have been some kind of distress of mind, concurrent with the effects of an old gun-shot wound, the ball still remaining somewhere in the body. My instructions were to remove this, at the express desire, as I understood, of the deceased, rather than to ascertain the precise cause of death. This, however, became apparent in the course of my search for the ball, which had enveloped itself in the muscular substance in the region of the heart, and was removed with difficulty. I have known cases of this kind, where anxiety has caused incurable cardiac derangement (deceased seems to have been actually sentenced to death for some military offence when on service in Flanders), and such mental strain would, of course, have been aggravated by the presence of a foreign object in that place. On arriving at my destination, a small village in a remote part of Sussex, I proceeded through the little orderly churchyard, where, however, the monthly roses were blooming all their own way among the formal white marble monuments of the wealthier people

74

of the neighbourhood. At one of these the masons were at work, picking and chipping in the otherwise absolute stillness of the summer afternoon. They were, in fact, opening the family burial place of the people who summoned me hither; and the workmen pointed out their abode, conspicuous on the slope beyond, towards which I bent my steps accordingly. I was conducted to a large upper room or attic, set freely open to sun and air, and found the body lying in a coffin, almost hidden under very rich-scented cut flowers, after a manner I have never seen in this country, except in the case of one or two Catholics laid out for burial. The mother of the deceased was present, and actually assisted my operations, amid such tokens of distress, though perfectly self-controlled, as I fervently hope I may never witness again. Deceased was in his twenty-seventh year, but looked many years younger: had, indeed, scarcely yet reached the full condition of manhood. The extreme purity of the outlines, both of the face and limbs, was such as is usually found only in quite early youth: the brow especially, under an abundance of fair hair, finely formed, not high, but arched and full, as is said to be the way with those who have the imaginative temper in excess. Sad to think that had he lived reason must have deserted that so worthy abode of it! I was struck by the great beauty of the organic developments, in the strictly anatomic sense; those of the throat and diaphragm in particular might have been modelled for a teacher of normal physiology, or a professor of design. The flesh was still almost as firm as that of a living person; as happens when, as in this case, death comes to all intents and purposes as gradually as in old age. This expression of health and life, under my seemingly merciless doings, together with the mother's distress, touched me to a degree very unusual, I conceive, in persons of my years and profession. Though I believed myself to be acting by his express wish, I felt like a criminal. The ball, a small one, much corroded with blood, was at length removed; and I was then directed to wrap it in a partly-printed letter, or other document, and place it in the breast-pocket of a faded and much-worn scarlet soldier's coat, put over the shirt which enveloped the body. The flowers were then hastily replaced, the hands and the peak of the handsome nose remaining visible among them; the wind ruffled the fair hair a little; the lips were still red. I shall not forget it. The lid was then placed on the coffin and screwed down in my presence. There was no plate or other inscription upon it.

*

Endnotes

References that can be found in an unabridged English dictionary or are otherwise self-explanatory are not included here unless they bear some special significance to the author or the text.

An earlier version of this book entitled *Three Imaginary Portraits* was published by Noumena Press in 2009. Since then, in 2014, Lene Østermark-Johansen's *Walter Pater: Imaginary Portraits* appeared as the first volume of the Jewelled Tortoise series of Critical Texts for the Modern Humanities Research Association. All of Pater's substantially completed *Imaginary Portraits* can be found there, supplemented by her copious, highly-detailed footnotes, which the present editor has taken the liberty of consulting on many occasions (particularly, in the absence of any specialized knowledge about The King's School at Canterbury, for "Emerald Uthwart") for the purpose of improving his own endnotes and filling in more than a few gaps. Those endnotes that specifically originate with Østermark-Johansen's edition have been noted. Those interested in reading more of Pater's *Portraits* would do well to consult her fine edition.

The Child in the House

In a letter dated 17 April 1878, Walter Pater wrote the following to George Grove, the editor of *Macmillan's Magazine*: "I send you by this post a M.S. entitled "The House and the Child," and I should be pleased if you should like to have it for *Macmillans'* [sic] *Magazine*. It is not, as you may perhaps fancy, the first part of a work of fiction, but is meant to be complete in itself; though the first of a series, as I hope, with some real kind of sequence in them, and which I should be glad to send to *you*. I call the M.S. a portrait, and mean readers, as they might do on seeing a portrait, to begin speculating—what came of him?"

The unsolicited manuscript was originally intended to appear "without signature," but Pater was eventually persuaded to identify himself as the author, and with a slight change of title it was published in the August 1878 issue (vol. 38, no. 226) under the heading "Imaginary Portraits I." Somewhat incongruously, "The Child in the House" did not appear in the 1887 collection entitled *Imaginary Portraits* as Pater felt that "it would need too many alterations." It was reprinted in 1895 along with "Emerald Uthwart" and other pieces in *Miscellaneous Studies*, a collection assembled by Charles Shadwell. The original periodical version of "The Child in the House," free of later revisions made by Shadwell, is the one reprinted here.

Based on the memories of his house at Enfield (a borough of Greater London), Pater called "The Child in the House" "the germinating, original, source, specimen, of all my *imaginative* work."

With regard to its influence, there is strong evidence to suggest that "The Child in the House" was a major—or quite possibly even indispensable—inspiration for Proust in his writing of *In Search of Lost Time*. See, for instance, *Proust: Swann's Way* (1989) by Sheila Stern, p. 40; Robert Fraser's *Proust and the Victorians* (1994), p. 247; and Emily Eells's essay, "'Influence occulte': the Reception of Pater's Works in France Before 1922," in *The Reception of Walter Pater in Europe* (2004), pp. 101-2.

4   *descent from Watteau*: though there are strong autobiographical elements in "The Child in the House," Pater was not related to the rococo painter. However, in his "A Prince of Court Painters" (1885), another *Imaginary Portrait*, there is a Jean-Baptiste Pater (referred to by his first name only, but whose identity can be inferred), an actual 18th century Flemish painter, and Watteau's only disciple. When asked if he was in fact related to him, Pater would always reply: "I think so; I believe so; I always say so."

5   Flos Parietis: commentators have been uncertain exactly what to make of this, an apparent play on words. Michael Levey in *The Case of Walter Pater* believes that the term is meant as "some sub-donnish joke," but is unable to shed further light. "*Flos Parietis*," as literally translated from the Latin, does in fact mean "wallflower," but is not a proper taxonym; the plant known by that name is of the genera Cheiranthus or Erysimum. A "wallflower" is also of course a "shy person," and would seem to come closer to what Pater might be referring to, but neither this nor the context in which it is mentioned again in "Emerald Uthwart" (see page 45) do much to clarify the matter. A third (though probably remote) possibility is that potassium nitrate or saltpeter was referred to by certain ancient naturalists as "*flos parietis*" because of the crystalline deposits the compound formed on cave walls, though how or if this fact might relate to any of the preceding definitions is unknown. The humor of the reference is perhaps better suited to a time when the study and knowledge of Latin and the classics were more widespread.

7   *"with lead in the rock for ever"*: "Oh that my words were now written! Oh that they were printed in a book! That they were graven with an iron pen and lead in the rock for ever!" Job 19:23-4.

8   *a mere childish* goûter: in France, the name for a small dessert or snack for children customarily served at about 4 o'clock in the afternoon.

80

the delightful chez soi: the feeling of being at home.

10   "*the lust of the eye*": "For all that is in the world, the lust of the flesh, and the lust of the eyes, and the pride of life, is not of the Father, but is of the world." 1 John 2:15–16.

Queen Marie Antoinette . . . we all remember David's drawing: see Plate I.

15   *the* Morgue *in Paris*: the *Morgue de Paris* was unusual in that it would publicly display unidentified corpses (usually murder victims or suicides, many of them pulled from the nearby Seine) as a means of assisting the police in ascertaining their identities. What began in the 18th century as a grim opportunity for public service on the part of the locals became over time little more than an attraction for tourists who wished to partake of the grisly spectacle. The morgue itself was moved on two occasions: once in 1804 to the Quai du Marché-Neuf on the Île de la Cité, and again in 1864 to the Quai de L'Archevêché to accomodate ever-larger crowds of visitors. Public viewing was finally prohibited in 1907 on grounds of "*hygiénisme moral*." Pater himself likely visited the Morgue while vacationing in Paris in August 1864.

16   *the "resurrection of the just" . . . Joshua's Vision in the Bible*: references to Luke 14:14 and Joshua 5:13-15, respectively.

18   *a "lively hope"*: "Blessed be the God and Father of our Lord Jesus Christ, which according to his abundant mercy hath begotten us again unto a lively hope by the resurrection of Jesus Christ from the dead." 1 Peter 1:3.

the wrestling angel grasped Jacob, how Jacob looked in his mysterious sleep . . . the hem of Aaron's vestment: references to Genesis 32:22-30, Genesis 28:12 (Jacob's Ladder), and Exodus 28:31-35, respectively.

Plate I: *Marie-Antoinette conduite à l'échafaud* (1793)
attributed to Jacques-Louis David

Plate II: *La falaise d'Étretat après l'orage* (1870)
by Gustave Courbet

19   *the deep, effusive unction of the House of Bethany*: a reference to Matthew 26:6-13 (Østermark-Johansen, 98).

An English Poet

Lawrence Evans, the editor of *The Letters of Walter Pater* (1970), has the following to say about "An English Poet:" "This 'portrait' breaks off abruptly in the middle of a sentence, whether because Pater never completed it or because the final pages have been lost or destroyed it seems impossible to determine ... it can be inferred that 'An English Poet' was begun in 1878; and [a subsequent letter] may suggest that it was still in progress as late as the autumn of 1881."

23   *the* Pays de Caux: a coastal area belonging to the Seine-Maritime département of Normandy, noted for its picturesque white chalk cliffs (see Plate II).

     the principle of the chez-soi: see second note to page 8.

25   *the gallant adventure which ended in loss of life there a month before*: in a footnote to the text, Mrs. Ottley writes: "Might this not refer to the Matterhorn disaster of July 14, 1865?" On that date the summit of the Matterhorn in the Pennine Alps was reached for the first time by a group of mountaineers led by Edward Whymper; during the descent, four of the seven climbers were killed.

27   *Hallstadt*: perhaps Hallstatt in Upper Austria, a small secluded village by a deep lake, bounded by high mountains (Østermark-Johansen, 104).

32   "il suffit que la pensée vous en soit venue pour que ma vie en demeure consolée et charmée": "that the thought of it came to you is enough to comfort and charm my life," a quote which can be found in Octave Feuillet's *Journal d'une femme* (1878). Another of Feuillet's works, *La Morte*, was positively reviewed by Pater for the December 1886 issue of *Macmillan's Magazine*, and was added to the second edition of *Appreciations, with an Essay on Style* (1890).

32   *the novelist with whom one lived in delicately haunted old New England mansions and Tuscan castles . . . one master of imaginative prose . . . a poet through whom the expression of being 'in the spirit' seemed clearly explained . . . another whose English birds' song was sweet alike over lawn and fen-land . . . another whose sacristy was a rich one . . .,* etc.: Østermark-Johansen believes it likely that in this passage Pater is referring to, respectively, Nathaniel Hawthorne, John Ruskin, Lord Byron, rural poet John Clare (1793-1864), and Samuel Taylor Coleridge, though the identities of the figures who "raised a Valhalla of wild romantic architecture" and "whose reflections were like lonely chapels" are less certain. Pater penned a short essay on Coleridge in 1865 that would later appear as one of his *Appreciations*.

      Browne, Webster, Chapman: Sir Thomas Browne, the author-physician; John Webster, the revenge tragedian; and George Chapman, the poet and translator, are meant. Browne was the subject of one of Pater's *Appreciations*.

33   *a great English poet*: Østermark-Johansen believes this to be a reference to Wordsworth, who was the also subject of one of Pater's *Appreciations*.

34   *"Words, words, words!" cries Hamlet*: a line from Act II, Scene II; there is no exclamation mark in the original.

      a world partly "out of joint": "Time is out of joint; O cursed spite,/That ever I was born to set it right!" *Hamlet*, Act I, Scene V.

35   *a certain hardness like that of a gem*: compare with "To burn always with this hard, gemlike flame, to maintain this ecstasy, is success in life," a famous quote from Pater's *The Renaissance: Studies in Art and Poetry* (1873).

36 *the action already within him of that strange malady . . .,* etc.: perhaps a reference to consumption or tuberculosis (Østermark-Johansen, 112).

Emerald Uthwart

One of the last *Imaginary Portraits* to be written by Pater before his death in 1894, "Emerald Uthwart" was, as Mrs. Ottley states in the introduction, inspired by his final visit to the King's School in the summer of 1891. The piece made its first appearance in two consecutive issues of *The New Review* in June and July 1892, and was also included in the collection *Miscellaneous Studies* (1895). As with "The Child in the House," the periodical version of the story is the one reprinted here.

Francis Fortescue Urquhart (1868-1934), known by the unfortunate nickname "Sligger," was a Tutorial Fellow of Balliol College, Oxford from 1896 until his death. During the time that Urquhart was an undergraduate at Balliol, Pater became friends with him, and it has been widely speculated that this "strikingly handsome young man" was the model for Emerald Uthwart.

41 *the great Dominican church . . . the impassioned work of Sodoma . . .* ætatis flore *. . . the University, famous early in the last century*: Pater is, firstly, referring to the Basilica di San Domenico in Siena in which the Italian Renaissance painter Giovanni Antonio Bazzi, also known as "Il Sodoma," decorated the Chapel of St. Catherine of Siena with a fresco depicting the saint fainting in ecstasy as she receives the Eucharist from an angel (Østermark-Johansen, 239).

The Latin phrase means "in the flower of youth."

The Università degli Studi di Siena, located in Tuscany, is a state-supported university dating to the mid-13th century noted for its schools of law and medicine (Østermark-Johansen, 239).

annos, menses, dies: "years, months, days."

Plate III: *The Dark Entry, Canterbury, from the Green Court* (1904) by Charles G. Harper

Plate IV: *The Norman Staircase* (1848)

42 *"Full of affections," observed, once upon a time, a great lover of boys and young men . . .,* etc.: an extended quote from a sermon by Thomas Arnold, the Headmaster of Rugby School and father of poet Matthew Arnold, entitled "Things Temporal and Things Eternal."

Chase Lodge: the name of an actual estate located in Enfield. Thomas Wright, in his *Life of Walter Pater*, claims that the name of Uthwart's home finds its origin in Chase Side, the location of Pater's home in Enfield. Uthwart's Chase Lodge, however, is apparently located in Chailey in East Sussex.

44 ablactatus a matre: "weaned from his mother."

45 Flos Parietis: see note to page 5.

"great matters": "Lord, my heart is not haughty, nor mine eyes lofty: neither do I exercise myself in great matters, or in things too high for me." Psalms 131:1.

48 *the "Green Court"*: a lawn lined with lime trees, situated at the center of the King's School, where cricket, races, and other athletic events take place (Østermark-Johansen, 245).

the "Angel Steeple": the spire of the central tower of the Cathedral, which was formerly adorned by the figure of a gilded angel that is no longer extant (Østermark-Johansen, 245).

49 *the "dark entry"*: a passage leading to Canterbury Cathedral where the ghost of poisoner Nell Cook, buried alive under one of its paving stones for her crime, was supposed to appear every Friday night (see Plate III).

the famous staircase of their school: the Norman Staircase, which dates to the 12th century. See Plate IV (Peter Henderson, the King's School Archivist, as referenced by Østermark Johansen, 246).

50   *It is good for a man that he bear the yoke in his youth . . .,*
      etc.: Lamentations 3:27-9.

      The aim of a veritable community, says Plato . . ., etc.: Pater
      further explored this idea in two essays from *Plato and
      Platonism* (1893): "Lacedæmon" and "The Republic"
      (Østermark-Johansen, 247).

      he felt the beauty of the ascêsis: a Greek word meaning
      "exercise," "training," or "discipline."

51   Introitum tuum, et exitum tuum, custodiat Dominus:
      "May the Lord keep thy coming in and thy going out."
      Psalm 120:8.

52   Preceptores, condiscipuli: teachers, fellow pupils.

53   *Ensigns,* Signiferi . . . in hac ecclesiâ pueri instituti: "The
      monument in the nave of the Cathedral to the memory
      of those of the thirty-first Regiment who died during
      the Sutlej campaign—still with tattered flags above it—
      mentions Ensigns Tritton and Jones. Tritton was an old
      King's Scholar" (Henderson as quoted by Østermark-
      Johansen, 249).
          Signiferi were standard bearers in the Roman legions.
          The Latin phrase means "boys educated in this
      church."

54   *"pause 'twixt cup and lip"*: an old saying, in full: "There's
      many a slip 'twixt the cup and the lip."

55   *to run a paper-chase*: "Paper-chases were King's School
      races run over, into, or through some thirty or forty
      ditches, ending with a swim in the Stour, the boys with
      their clothes on, completed with a full meal and a game
      of bowls at the Ferry hostelry, and then a walk home
      in the evening" (Henderson as quoted by Østermark-
      Johansen, 251).

88

Sidus Cantiorum: "the comet of Kent." Apparently an allusion to *Sidus Iulium*, a comet that appeared shortly after Caesar's death in 44 BC, believed to be a manifestation of the recently assassinated statesman's soul (Østermark-Johansen, 251).

"*the masters of those who know*": "the *master* of those who know" (*il maestro di color chi sanno*), a reference to Aristotle made in Canto IV of Dante's *Inferno*.

56   "*which no one knoweth, saving he that receiveth it*": "To him that overcometh will I give to eat of the hidden manna, and will give him a white stone, and in the stone a new name written, which no man knoweth saving he that receiveth it." Revelation 2:17.

57   ἡ πτεροῦ δύναμις, *says Plato, in the* Phædrus: (transliteration: hê pterou dynamis) "the power of the wing." The wing, in this instance, is a near-divine attribute of the soul as described by Socrates in his dialogue with Phaedrus.

58   *like* Tryphon, Son of Eutychos: see Plate V. This sepulchral frieze or stele, dating to the 4th century BC, originally formed part of the Temple of Apollo located in the ancient Greek city of Phigaleia. In his right hand the figure of Tryphon carries a strigil, which is a small metal tool used for scraping sweat and dirt from the body. The cloak draped over his left shoulder, known as a chlamys, was worn by Greek soldiers of that era. Pater also makes reference to this sculpture in an essay entitled "The Age of Athletic Prizemen" (1894).

59   *the "Warriors' Chapel"*: St. Michael's Chapel, located in the southwest transept of Canterbury Cathedral, houses the tombs of Lady Margaret Holland, at whose direction the chapel was built in 1439, and her two husbands John Beaufort, the Earl of Somerset, and Thomas, Duke of Clarence, both of whom fought in the Hundred Years War (Henderson as referenced by Østermark-Johansen, 256).

Plate V: *Tryphon, son of Eutychos* (c. 5th century BC)

60   The first part of "Emerald Uthwart," as presented in *The New Review*, ends here.

       "Victors" of the school: an honorific title dating to the 17th century bestowed upon " . . . two of your number who deserve the chief praise for good character and learning. These two shall, in virtue of their title of 'Victors' in the school, receive this wreath of laurel as their due reward . . . it is a prize not to be lightly regarded, but to be coveted beyond all others, inasmuch as it confers on the 'Victors' not only a genuine honour, but also various accompanying privileges" (the *Orationes & Carmina aliaque Exercitia* as quoted by Østermark-Johansen, 257).

       that place in Homer, where the soul of the lad Elpenor . . . entreats Ulysses for due burial rites . . ., etc.: a scene from Book XI of *The Odyssey*.

62   *a "passman"*: One who obtains a degree without honors. Rather surprisingly, Pater only received a second-class degree from Oxford (Østermark-Johansen, 258).

63   *the military life that intruded itself so oddly, during the Civil War . . .*, etc.: though the town of Oxford sided with Cromwell and the Parliamentarians during the English Civil War, Charles I took refuge at Christ Church College in Oxford approximately nine months after fleeing from London, and remained there from 1642-1646. The King assembled the Oxford Parliament (also known as the "Mongrel Parliament") in 1644 in the college's Great Hall; that year also saw the first of three sieges against city, which finally surrendered to the Roundheads in 1646 (Østermark-Johansen, 259).

       young Colonel Windebank: a Royalist soldier and son of Sir Francis Windebank, Charles I's Secretary of State. During the first English Civil War, Colonel Francis Windebank was made governor of Bletchingdon Park near Oxford, which he surrendered to Cromwell's

91

forces without a fight in April 1645, a decision that led to a charge of treason and his execution by firing squad a month later. The ghost of Colonel Widebank is said to haunt Dead Man's Walk, south of Merton College, Oxford, the place of his execution.

63 fastus *he terms it*: this is quite possibly a misprint in the text from *The New Review* that remained uncorrected in *Miscellaneous Studies*; the Latin word *fastus* means "calendar," which in this context makes no apparent sense. If, however, the word *fastosus*, meaning "pride" or "haughtiness," is put in its place, the statement becomes more comprehensible.

64 *they set out with as little delay as possible for Flanders*: Uthwart and Stokes have presumably joined the British contingent of the Army of Flanders led by Wellington, and are going off to fight the French during the period of Napoléon's return from exile known as The Hundred Days (20 March-8 July 1815, actually 111 days in total). The Emperor was defeated at Waterloo on 18 June, abdicated four days later, and surrendered to the English on 15 July. Louis XVIII's restoration on 8 July brought the Hundred Days to an end.

65 pièce justificative: supporting documentation.

68 locus standi: literally, "place to stand;" it is the right to challenge a legal decision or to be heard before a court.

73 pessimi exempli: the worst examples.

Selected Bibliography
and Further Reading

Bann, Stephen: *The Reception of Walter Pater in Europe* (Thoemmes Continuum, 2004) ISBN-13: 9780826468468.

Benson, A.C.: *Walter Pater* (The Macmillan Company, 1906).

Brake & Small (eds.): *Pater in the 1990s* (ELT Press, 1991) ISBN-13: 9780944318058.

Crinkley, Richmond: *Walter Pater: Humanist* (University Press of Kentucky, 1970).

Donoghue, Denis: *Walter Pater: Lover of Strange Souls* (Knopf, 1995) ISBN-13: 9780679437536.

Evans, Lawrence (ed.): *The Letters of Walter Pater* (The Clarendon Press, 1970) ISBN-13: 9780198124061.

Greenslet, Ferris: *Walter Pater* (William Heinemann, 1904).

Levey, Michael: *The Case of Walter Pater* (Thames and Hudson, 1978) ISBN-13: 9780500011935.

McKenzie, Gordon: *The Literary Character of Walter Pater* (University of California Press, 1967).

Monsman, Gerald Cornelius: *Pater's portraits: Mythic Pattern in the Fiction of Walter Pater* (Johns Hopkins Press, 1967).

——————————: *Walter Pater* (Twayne Publishers, 1977).

——————————: *Walter Pater's Art of Autobiography* (Yale University Press, 1980) ISBN-13: 9780300025330.

Østermark-Johansen, Lene (ed.): *Walter Pater: 'Imaginary Portraits'* (Modern Humanities Research Association, 2014) ISBN-13: 9781907322556.

Shuter, William F.: *Rereading Walter Pater* (Cambridge University Press, 1997) ISBN-13: 9780521572217.

Wright, Samuel: *A Bibliography of the Writings of Walter H. Pater* (Garland Pub., 1975).

Wright, Thomas: *The Life of Walter Pater* (Haskell House, 1969).

www.ingramcontent.com/pod-product-compliance
Lightning Source LLC
Chambersburg PA
CBHW072010170626
46813CB00005B/2101